I'm a local indie author, now using the name Ali Ryecart.
www.ryecart.com

A CHRISTMAS WEDDING
A SNOWY LONDON LOVE STORY

A E RYECART

Ali x

To find out more about the author visit:

www.aeryecart.com

Disclaimer

This book is a work of fiction. No part may be reproduced, by any means, without the written permission of the author. Names and characters, businesses, organisations, products or services and places and events are either the product of the author's imagination or are used fictitiously. Any resemblance to actual persons, living or dead, is entirely coincidental.

All trademarks are the property of their respective owners. This work contains descriptions of a sexual nature and is not intended for readers under the age of 18 years.

Copyright © 2019 A E Ryecart
All rights reserved

For Mark

Writing a book is a lone endeavour, but the finished product is a team effort. Beta readers, editors, cover artists and more: thank you.

But I'll end where I started, with Mark, for being unstinting in your support and encouragement.

CHAPTER ONE

"We've made a mistake."

"What are you talking about?" Jack pulled his attention away from the TV and stared down at Rory, nestling in his lap. His fiancé's comment had come out of the blue.

"About getting married. At Christmas, I mean. Not about getting married."

Rory stared up at him with anxiety-filled eyes.

"No, Ro. It's the best time. We chose the date for a reason. Remember?"

Rory pushed himself out of Jack's lap, sat up, and shifted around so he was looking Jack square in the face. Jack paused the drama unfolding on the TV to give all his attention to the potential drama sitting next to him.

"I know, and there's nobody who understands that more than me. This time of year, it's so significant to us. But we should have thought about it a bit more, you know? Thought about the practicalities. I mean, this is our first real Christmas at The Bakehouse."

Rory paused, his hands twisting and knotting together in his lap. Jack pushed away the dark hair that had flopped across Rory's brow, and waited.

"I never, ever thought the bakery would take off like it has," Rory said, looking up at Jack. "It's been everything I'd hoped for and more, but we're run off our feet. We've got a list as long as your arm for private orders, with more coming in, on top of the day-to-day running. And there are all the wedding preparations, with only two weeks to do it in."

"Hey." Jack pulled Rory into his chest.

Rory's resistance was small but there, his muscles stiff and tight with worry.

"Ro?" Jack's voice dipped, became deeper, more gravelly. Rory flopped against him, and Jack tightened his hold, ready as always to take Rory's weight. "I can't imagine us marrying at any other time. Can you?"

Rory muttered something that sounded like *no*, and snuggled closer into Jack as though seeking warmth and comfort.

And no wonder.

Jack closed his eyes. Two years before, and a freezing cold night just days before Christmas. A hungry and homeless boy huddled on his doorstep... he shook his head, pushing back at the crashing memories. It was a miracle that had saved them both. Jack forced his eyes open and gazed down at the tumble of Rory's dark hair. His man was safe and warm in his arms, and always would be. Jack breathed in deep, willing his racing heart rate to slow and calm.

"It just feels so overwhelming," Rory whispered. "The business, I love it so much and wouldn't want it any other way, but it takes up so much of my energy. Perhaps we were being overambitious, trying to fit in the wedding—"

"But that would be the case for any time of year, wouldn't it?"

"Yes, I suppose—no, not suppose. You're right. I know you are."

Jack hugged him in closer as his brain whirled and buzzed. Nerves, that was all it was. The business was demanding, no two ways about it: early starts, late nights, non-stop for six days a week. It was everything they'd worked for, had exceeded their expectations, but the hard work took its toll. And on top of it all, a Christmas wedding.

"I'm just feeling the stress," Rory murmured.

Jack eased Rory into sitting up. He pushed aside the hank of dark hair that had once again fallen over Rory's eyes, earning himself a smile.

"Weddings are always like this, whenever they are. They're always stressful, you can't escape that. Which is why we agreed that Mum would be our wedding planner."

Rory nodded, but his arms hugging themselves around his middle and the bite down on his lower lip gave him away.

Jack's brow tightened as he pulled his brows inwards. Something else was bothering Rory, something that was more than just pre-wedding jitters.

"Ro?"

Rory didn't answer, and worry crept across Jack's skin.

"Your mum's doing everything," Rory said at last, unwinding his arms from his middle, his glance flickering from his lap to Jack, and back again. "When she offered I jumped at the chance, so don't get me wrong. I appreciate it and went along with it but…"

"But?"

Rory golf balled his cheeks, letting go of a long breath as he met Jack's eyes.

"I just feel I should be more involved than I am. I know I stepped back, but — but it's like decisions have been made that I've — that we've — had no part in. I know how ungrateful that sounds, especially when most couples would be doing a happy dance that somebody else was taking on all the work. I sound so petty and I don't mean it to be..."

But... Reassurance. If that's what Rory needed, that would be what Rory got.

Jack took Rory's hands in his and swept his thumbs across his knuckles.

"It's a simple wedding, just as we agreed it would be. Just us, immediate family, and our friends. But even a simple wedding takes a lot of organising, and there's always last-minute stuff to see to. A bit like baking, eh?" Jack shook out Rory's hands and earned himself a wry smile. "All those fancy cupcakes you bake, with the weird-flavoured buttercream icing on top—"

Rory huffed, but it didn't disguise the smile in his voice. "My flavoured frostings are *not* weird. The proof of that is in how well they sell."

"Yes, but the cake itself is simple, isn't it? What takes the time, and is the clever part, is getting the buttercream just right, piping it into a perfect peak, and then adding all the little flourishes that give them the wow factor. A wedding's no different, whether it's small and low-key like ours or a big society affair—"

"Are you saying ours isn't a society wedding?" Rory

quirked his brow as he climbed into Jack's lap and wound his arms around his neck.

Now, this was better, this was the Rory he wanted back. Jack's dick agreed as it twitched beneath the layer of denim.

"It'll be better than any society wedding because it'll have—*oh*..."

The flick of Rory's tongue around his ear and the light scraping of teeth on the nervy, sensitive skin just beneath the lobe were making him forget all about weddings and bakeries and cupcake analogies...

"Been to a lot of society weddings, have you?"

"Hmm? What?" Jack scrambled to catch up. "Yes, lots. I was a page boy at—ow!" Jack yelped when Rory bit hard on his ear.

"Page boys. Your mum suggested we have page boys. And flower girls. Did you know? I think she was keen for Hugo and Henry to play a role."

Jack blinked hard. "She wanted the Monsters to be page boys?" His dick deflated at the thought of his adorable but undeniably badly-behaved young nephews dressed as Little Lord Fauntleroy. "No, I didn't. When was this? You didn't say."

"At the beginning. She phoned — me — when you were — out." Rory said in between landing kisses and tiny nips on Jack's throat. "She was in full flow. Almost unstoppable. It was bloody scary, but I had to say no. She was pissed off, I could tell."

"You should have told me, Ro. I could have had a word, told her to go easy." And stay within the remit. Where did page boys and flower girls figure in a simple wedding? "Don't keep stuff from me, okay?"

Rory slipped from Jack's lap and took up his former position, cuddling into Jack's side.

"Perhaps I'm just being overly touchy."

"Not about page boys and flower girls you're not. You were right to put your foot down. Any other surprises for me?"

Rory shook his head.

Jack ran his fingers through Rory's thick, dark hair. He wished Rory had said something to him at the time. To him, his mum was just that — Mum. But to Rory, his future mother-in-law was still very much Lady Diana De Lacy. Strong-willed and determined, she was a force to be reckoned with, but Rory had stood up to that and come off the better, and not for the first time. Still, it would have taken every scrap of Rory's courage.

Simple, tasteful, low-key. Those were the ground rules they had set down, months and months before. And his mother had embraced them. Hadn't she?

There had been the announcement in The Times, of course. That went without saying. And his and

Rory's suits were bespoke with one final fitting yet to take place… weren't these things the ordinary, normal stuff of weddings? Or at least the weddings he'd been to, but then most probably didn't attend the nuptials of Sir this, Lady that, or the Honourable the other…

"Are you sorry we're not getting married in Polton Lacy? I mean really? I know it's a tradition for your family."

Polton Lacy, the tiny Devonshire village and ancestral home of the De Lacys. Jack gathered his thoughts before he answered.

"Tradition's a good thing, goodness knows I was brought up steeped in it, but sometimes you have to break the mould. And we're hardly a traditional couple, are we? Eh?" Jack gave Rory a small nudge, and smiled. "Our life is here in London, and we agreed it felt right to get married here, but we couldn't have got married in the village in any case — a same sex marriage in St Peter's? The ladies of the Friends of St Peter's would have a fit of the vapours, even if we were allowed to get married in the church. Which we aren't."

"Does that bother you? That we can't?"

Jack's brow scrunched in thought. "It's wrong on so many levels that we're barred from marrying in church, but would I want us to have a church wedding, even if we could? No. I wouldn't. It's right for some, but not for us."

"I think so, too." Rory nodded, and Jack smiled.

He tightened his arms around Rory, and stared at the mute, flickering TV screen as his thoughts drifted.

The non-existent options for getting married in the village had been something of a godsend, but he'd kept that thought to himself. A De Lacy wedding, in the heart of De Lacy country, the village turning out to gawp, a photographer from the county newspaper... to him, it was nothing; he'd seen it all before, but for Rory? Getting married in London solved all of it in one sweep. They'd even set their hearts on the quirky little hotel not far from the bakery, but it had been fully booked for functions throughout December. His mother's suggestion of the smart West End hotel, all pale lemon walls and ornate plastered ceilings, had been a beautiful alternative, they'd both agreed. Okay, its walls weren't crowded with eclectic artwork, and there were no lava lamps...

"What's that?"

Too wrapped up in his thoughts, Jack had missed what Rory was saying.

"...a white carriage pulled by six ponies. She just said the Daimler was more appropriate."

"Err...?"

"I said we should have a carriage to take us to the

venue. I think she thought I was being serious. I was joking, but it fell a bit flat."

Jack snorted. She'd have been horrified and would have been imagining something from The Best Worst Wedding show on TV. If she watched such a thing, which Jack doubted.

"When she went through the canapés to have with drinks before the wedding breakfast, I said I'd also like some of those mini cones of fish and chips, and mini burgers. She suggested they wouldn't go with the wine, but she was forgetting I'm a trained chef. And I've completed a wine tasting course."

Rory huffed, and he had every right to. But Jack didn't remember any mention of this...

"Where was I when you were locking horns with my mum?"

Lifting his head, Rory's lips curved in a wry smile. "This was all weeks and weeks ago. I did tell you. She said they'd be a bit messy to eat. Couldn't really deny that, so I just left the whole thing. The menu's gorgeous, no denying. So I guess your mum was right after all." Rory lowered his head and carried on snuggling. "It'll be beautiful and stylish and lovely. I know it will."

Jack's stomach clenched. Yes, it would be all those things and more, but would it be the simple day he and Rory had imagined, almost a year before? What else had he missed, in his unthinking, uncritical conviction that his mother would arrange the perfect wedding for him and Rory? What battles had Rory fought for them to have the day they wanted? With just two weeks to go before their Christmas Eve wedding, it was too late to change anything other than the simplest, most superficial arrangements.

"Ro?" Jack said, nudging Rory so that he sat up.

"What?" Rory tilted his head.

"It will be perfect, I promise you. It will be perfect and beautiful and everything beyond and in between. Because it'll be our wedding, you and me surrounded by the people we love and the people who love us in return. That's what matters, and that we say our vows in front of all the people who are important to us. Everything else, it's just window dressing."

Jack shifted and placed his palms on Rory's cheeks, cupping his fiancé's face, holding him still as he brushed his lips to Rory's. His heart twisted as Rory's sigh shivered against him.

Jack let his hands fall away. Their wedding was supposed to be a joyous thing, an event to mark not just how far they had come, but also the start of the next stage in their lives together.

"I know, and I also know I should be grateful for all the work your mum's putting in, instead of bitching about canapés."

"We could have bags of chips with battered sausage and mushy peas from the chippie for all I care. No second thoughts?" Jack asked after a tiny pause.

Rory's eyes widened. Jack didn't expect him to glance away, to hesitate, to lick his lips before he answered. He didn't expect any of it, but it didn't stop the breath catching in his throat and the wild pummelling of his heart when Rory stared and didn't answer.

"Do you really think I could ever have second thoughts?"

"No, but—"

"Listen to me, Jack."

Rory trailed his fingers down Jack's cheek and along his jawbone, and Jack instinctively pressed into Rory's touch, the comforter turned the comforted.

"Everything that's happened to me, every cold bad thing, it's like it all happened for a reason. And that reason's you, Jack. Everything that's happened has brought me to you. Our wedding is the affirmation of that."

Rory looked down, dipping his head forward, but it didn't hide the scrunch of his nose or muffle his small sniff. Jack's heart clenched; Rory was fighting hard to hold back his tears.

"Ro—"

"No, don't say anything. Just—just accept that."

They settled back into the sofa, neither saying anything more about the wedding as though by mutual yet unspoken consent. Snuggling together, Jack released the pause button on the remote, and the frozen actors sprang into life. But he saw none of it, his thoughts turning over and over as he swept his fingers through Rory's warm and silky hair.

CHAPTER TWO

Every time Rory walked into The Bakehouse he had the urge to pinch himself.

It didn't matter that it was 5:30 am and he'd left Jack sleeping in bed, or that the still-black sky was trying its hardest to snow and the wind was sharp and biting. None of it mattered, not one bit.

First thing, when it was just him alone in the shop, this was his time. Everything quiet, calm, and still, it was as if The Bakehouse was taking a moment, holding its breath, a calm before the onslaught of custom that would start from the moment the sign on the door was switched from closed to open at 8:00 am and the door unlocked, never stopping until the final customers were said goodbye to with a smile and a wave. At 5:00 pm, the door was shut, the lock turned, and the sign switched back to closed. And it all began again the following day.

Rory loved it.

But he loved this quiet time, too, a time to be savoured.

How have we achieved so much in just a year? It was a question he asked himself over and over. Hard work, his and Jack's. And not forgetting their tiny staff of two, Mabel and Lance. Everybody had pulled together, determined to make the bakery the huge success it was. But most of all, it had been because of Jack's unstinting belief in what they were doing, Jack's unstinting belief in *him*.

At the back of the shop, most of the space was taken up by the kitchen where all the baking magic happened. Behind the kitchen, a small area had been turned into a storeroom, and within that, an even smaller space had been hived off just big enough to make tea and coffee. A fold-up table and stacking chairs were crammed into the corner. It was just as well they took breaks in rotation because if they were all wedged into the tiny space, Rory doubted they'd ever get out.

Rory took his coffee into the public area of the bakery and switched on the tree lights, and those draped around the rest of the shop, illuminating The Bakehouse in all its Christmas glory.

Deep blue fairy lights wound their way along the edge of the counter, around the window and the large antique-looking mirror that took up much of one of the walls. Rory's lips lifted in a wicked grin when his gaze fell on the small tree set up in the bow window. He and Jack had had a lot of fun decorating the tree, a couple of Sunday afternoons before, the only day in the week the bakery was closed for business.

The little plastic tree, like the one he and Jack had at home, wasn't about stylish good taste. It was kitsch, camp, and over the top all at once. Every spindly branch was heaped with bright garlands of multi-coloured tinsel and weighed down with gingerbread men. All men, all wearing harnesses and all sporting droopy moustaches. Of course, he and Jack knew, that but anybody else would think the harnesses were braces and the droopy moustaches wide smiles. When Mabel had come in to work the following day, she'd examined the dangling men, her only comment an already arched brow arching higher into her extravagant 1960s beehive.

Rory's gaze drifted upwards to the ceiling where Christmas stars, Santas, and reindeer were suspended, twisting, turning, then twisting back in the imperceptible air current. They were the same decorations that had hung from the ceiling a year before, when they'd opened The Bakehouse's door for the first time. A tingle danced its way down Rory's backbone. How could he have known where he and Jack would be, a year on? His gaze drifted to the shelves and bread racks lining the wall behind the counter.

"Hello, Doris."

The doll, once a toy soldier, stared down at him from her cushion of rainbow feathers. Doris, the drag queen Christmas fairy, had been one of Jack's Christmas traditions long before he had come into Jack's life.

The memory was as warm and sweet as a mince pie straight from the oven. Two years before, taking refuge against the freezing winter, wrapped up in the warmth not just in Jack's cosy home but in the warmth of his friendship, too. Friendship that for Rory had already been turning to love.

He blinked to clear his misted vision, which had made the lights twinkling in the shop take on an even softer glow. They had decorated Jack's little Christmas tree together. The memory was so crisp Rory could almost touch it.

Together, they'd heaped the tree with mismatched decorations. Laughing and joking, they'd drunk too many eggnogs and got a little tipsy. For a while they'd made themselves forget that Jack had been fighting the heartache of betrayal from those he should have been able to trust with his life, and that *he* would soon be leaving the magic of Christmas behind to take up, once more, his hopeless, wretched life back on the streets.

Rory rubbed a hand over his face, wiping away the dampness filling his eyes. He wouldn't think about what his life had been like before Jack. He'd never forget it, but he wouldn't *think* about it.

But now Doris was *their* tradition as she'd taken her place centre stage on one of the shelves, perched year-round high on her feathery throne. Rory frowned, and his lips twisted in a downwards curve. He and Jack had yet to drag their tree from its hiding place at the back of a deep cupboard, along with the bag of beaten and battered decorations. No tree, no baubles and pinecones, the cards they'd received sitting in a pile by the TV. It didn't matter what else was happening they needed to put that right, and fast. They'd met at Christmas, they'd opened the shop at Christmas, and they were to be married at Christmas. Christmas was them, as they were Christmas.

Rory took another sip of his coffee, but what was left was hardly even tepid.

How long have I been daydreaming for?

With another busy day ahead, the answer could only be *too long*.

It wasn't just the remains of the unappetising coffee that reminded Rory he needed to get on, but the heavy bang on the door as well.

Rory's eyes widened. How hadn't he noticed that the thin on-off sleet that had accompanied the short walk from the flat had turned into fat flakes of snow? Abandoning his near-empty mug, he dashed to the door, unlocked it — and was nearly thrown off his feet when it was flung open by a bundled-up ball of leopard skin print faux fur.

"Frigging hell, it's bloody freezing out there."

The faux fur coat was peeled off, followed by a fruit-patterned scarf, and a black hat with plastic cherries bobbing around its brim. From under the layers, a short young woman emerged, dressed in a bright pink 1960s shift dress decorated with prints of apples, oranges, and bananas. In the midst of winter, she was a sunny, summery fruit salad. On the end of her fishnet-clad legs were a pair of flower-patterned Doctor Martens, cartoonishly large against her dainty frame.

Dainty? Rory swallowed a snort.

"I'm thinking of introducing a uniform policy." Rory struggled to keep his face straight. "Black trousers, black polo shirts with The Bakehouse's logo subtly and tastefully embroidered on the chest. What do you think?" Rory knew exactly what Mabel would think.

"Why be boring? Who wants to blend in when you can stand out? You wanna be like all those high-street chains?" She raised a perfectly shaped brow as she looked him up and down in mock disdain. Rory grinned. She wasn't expecting an answer he wasn't going to give. No, he wasn't going to introduce uniform policy, and Mabel knew it as well as he did.

"I'll get us some coffee, shall I, boss?" Mabel stomped into the back of the shop without waiting for an answer.

"You looked like you were away with the fairies when I banged on the door," Mabel said, handing over a coffee a couple of minutes later. "Thinking about the wedding, were you?" She smiled, softening the take-on-all-comers expression that lurked on her face for much of the time.

Rory shrugged. "No. Just enjoying some peace and quiet before the mayhem starts again."

They sipped their coffee, the silence comfortable and companionable.

"I almost got married, a couple of years back. Did a runner on the day. All hell broke loose."

Rory's jaw dropped as his mug began to slip from his hands. He tightened his grasp to stop it crashing to the floor.

"What?"

It wasn't just that Mabel had been a runaway bride, but that she had been on the verge of getting married at all that had made him gawp. Matrimony seemed too conventional for a woman who dressed like a Motown diva and wore a hat covered in plastic cherries.

"Got scared. Me and Keith, we weren't right for each other but that's another story. But it was the whole circus that sprung into life as soon as we told our families. We wanted the local register office, our parents, and a handful of mates followed by a piss-up in our local pub."

She huffed and shook her head as she stared out into the shop.

"No way that was going to happen. My future mother-in-law, it was like she was getting married, not me and Keith. She became this kind of wedding monster truck, driving through and flattening everything in front of her. We were glad she was taking on the work, or at first, but it became a friggin' nightmare. And we couldn't stop her. Nobody could. Before we knew it, the register office and local boozer had turned into a posh hotel, and I was going for dress fittings to be made to look like a puffed-up meringue."

"But you must have been able to say no, that it wasn't what you wanted?"

Rory licked his suddenly dry lips. The taste of coffee was sour in his mouth, and he put his mug aside.

"You'd think, as I'm not shy in coming forward." Mabel gave a twisted, humourless smile. "Problem was, Keith's parents were paying for it. They were well off.

Me and Keith didn't have too much spare cash, but even if we had, neither of us wanted to blow it on a flashy wedding, and my mum couldn't help because she never had two pennies to rub together."

"So it made it hard, saying something and—and putting the brakes on?" Why did his words feel like dust balls in his mouth? Rory tried to swallow, and couldn't.

Mabel nodded. "Hard doesn't describe it. A strong willed would-be mother-in-law with the bit between her teeth is impossible to stop when she's speeding towards you with table linen swatches in half a dozen colours in one hand and a selection of dinky little canapés to choose from in the other. Before I knew it, I was standing in front of over a hundred people, most of them old relatives of Keith's even he'd forgotten about, looking like a cross between a drag queen fairy princess and a cotton wool ball."

"And you ran away? From the altar?" Rory croaked.

Mabel threw back the last of her coffee and pushed herself away from the end of the counter where they were leaning.

"Yep. Just knew I had to escape and leave everything behind."

"And Keith? What about him?" Rory stared at Mabel, not able to drag his eyes away.

Mabel smiled. "We reconciled, after a time. He realised he'd had a lucky escape, too. He's married to a doctor, now, with a baby on the way I heard. It all turned out for the best, in the end." Her smile turned into a laugh. "But don't you be getting any ideas. You and Jack are perfect together. I'd say cute if I didn't know you'd tut and roll your eyes."

When Rory didn't answer Mabel stopped, mugs in her hands and in mid-turn towards the back of the shop. The shadowed light cast by the Christmas lights didn't disguise the concerned wrinkling of her brow, of the disturbing question in her eyes.

"Rory? You're not...?"

Rory, not the usual *boss*. She only used his name when she had something serious to say, all flippancy and light-heartedness stripped away.

"Having doubts? About Jack? No." If he was sure about anything in his life, he was sure about that, *but*... "What you said, about the wedding growing into something you'd never even considered, it struck a chord I suppose."

"The future mother-in-law from hell?"

He wouldn't put it quite like that, but Diana had taken the reins of his and Jack's wedding and was steering it with as much confidence and skill as she did one of the many horses kept at the Devonshire estate.

"It feels like such a big deal. Not marrying Jack, but marrying into the De Lacy family."

He shouldn't be telling Mabel this. She was his employee, but her confession, never guessed at, had loosened his own. He needed to talk, and in the warm and quiet bakery, before the day descended and swept them along like a fast-flowing river, he found his confessional.

"Ah, the regal, aristocratic family with the country pile and horses and servants. The weight of expectation and the fear you're stepping into shoes that feel too big. I get it. Keith's family weren't in the same league as Jack's, but they were still a million miles above me. They had a swimming pool and a hot tub, and a villa in Spain, near Alicante."

Mabel chuckled, and Rory joined in. Diana would have views about Spanish villas and hot tubs.

Rory's laugh faded. "I love Jack's family, I honestly do — and I'm very close to his sister — but I still get overawed when I think of all that history and tradition. And I feel so small against all that." He looked down. Adopted by a couple who lost interest in him years before, with no idea who his natural parents were. As much as he tried to stand tall in front of the De Lacys and all their surety of where they had come from and where they were going, sometimes it was hard.

"Why should you feel small? Look at everything

you've achieved. Look around you, at this amazing business you've built up. You and Jack. You two are a partnership, in more ways than one, and that's what you need to remember." Mabel gave his arm a reassuring squeeze. "It's easy for me to say don't think about his family, but then I'm not marrying into that level of posh," she said with a gentle laugh. "Jack's who you need to concentrate on because you're marrying *him*. It doesn't matter who his family is, how loaded they are, or how many ponies they have."

Rory laughed. They had more than ponies in their stables in the family home down in Devon. And yes, Mabel was right in what she said. It was Jack he was marrying and making a new life with. And Jack's parents were happy for them both, he knew they were. Yet despite them welcoming him into their lives, there was a tiny worm of doubt crawling deep in his stomach that maybe, just maybe, Sir Roger and Lady Diana De Lacy might, just, harbour the unspoken thought that their beloved son could have done so much better for himself than an adopted kid from a dull commuter town.

"That man loves the bones of you," Mabel said quietly.

Rory glanced across, the softness and dreaminess in her eyes not obscured by the shadows cast by the fairy lights or the winter dawn reaching in through the windows.

"Everytime he looks at you, awe, wonder, and sheer love shine out of him. That's rare, and it's all that matters, or it should be. What's his family, up against that? Even if they have got a field full of friggin' ponies."

Mabel's wide-mouthed, scarlet-lipsticked grin, and conspiratorial exaggerated wink, broke through the little bubble they had found themselves in — as did the sudden hammering on the door. They both turned to see Lance's face, partially swathed in a bright yellow scarf, squashed up against the glass, and Jack walking towards the shop, a few yards behind.

"Well, it looks like the rest of the cavalry's arrived," Mabel said as she went to let Lance in. "Then I'll get the muffins out front, shall I, boss?"

CHAPTER THREE

"Would you like to try one of our Christmas pudding muffins? They're a limited edition," Jack added, at the same time he leant forward and held out a Santa gingerbread man to the customer's young daughter. "Here you go, something for the prettiest young lady in the shop." The little girl smiled shyly and looked up at her mother, hope written across her face that she'd be allowed the festive treat.

The woman nodded, to both her daughter and Jack, then adding not one muffin but two, plus three mini Yule logs to her existing order of half a dozen mince pies and a loaf of sourdough.

She was a new customer, he knew. She'd called into The Bakehouse earlier in the week, and Jack had overheard her talking to Mabel, telling her she'd just moved to the area. Another young, affluent family.

Soon, they wouldn't be able to move for Range Rovers, vegan cafés, and yoga classes. Mother and child, all smiles, left. Please the child, please mother. Jack was confident the bakery had not one but two new fans.

The lunchtime rush was over, which meant The Bakehouse was quiet. Jack eyed the five people queuing at the counter. Quiet was a relative term. All except one were regular customers; he knew most by name and what they were going to order before they asked. Most were like the woman with the young daughter: well off and willing to spend their very generous disposable income in The Bakehouse and the other independents which had sprung up in the area. It was exactly the client base he and Rory had set out to attract when they had opened up a year before.

Jack dealt with the small queue before he was free to set about tidying up the display counter.

He'd never imagined he'd enjoy working in a shop and dealing with the public. Jack smiled as he rearranged the packets of toffee and ginger cookies, their Christmas star-patterned paper bags tied at the top with an extravagant red-and-green bow. They were a best seller, and Mabel was in the back, bagging up another batch which had cooled from being cooked that morning. The warm aroma filled the shop, rich and heady with sweet spices; if he breathed in deep, he was sure he'd go a little dizzy and his legs would buckle beneath him. But Rory's baking had a habit of doing that, and it was why the shop had become the wild success it had.

It wasn't long before a fresh influx of customers came in. Jack glanced at his watch, but he already knew the time. Three o'clock, and that meant mostly young mothers with their kids, just picked up from the local Montessori and other private pre-schools.

Jack didn't miss the glances one or two threw around. He knew what they were hoping to spot: tables. Little, round café tables.

He smiled, chatting away, accepting but not returning the gentle flirting of the last woman in the queue, a tall and attractive blonde who let her gaze linger a beat too long as she twisted a strand of long hair around her red-nailed finger.

Jack stifled a groan as he forced his smile to stay in place. He thought all their customers knew he and Rory were together and about to be married. He'd mentioned it to Mabel a couple or so months before, after the blonde had added a simper to her winsome smile. Mabel had laughed, loud and raucous, before she'd disappeared into the kitchen, shaking her head and muttering something inaudible as she went.

"You really should try and add some tables and chairs, and install a coffee machine," the blonde said, twirling her hair and smiling.

"It's certainly something to think about," Jack said as he bagged up The Bakehouse's signature bake of chocolate, caramel, and sour cherry brownie and handed it across. His answer was cheery and noncommittal, but it was exactly what he and Rory *should* be thinking about, and soon. The woman waved goodbye, wiggling her scarlet nails, and left.

He dealt with one customer after the next, smiling, laughing, chatting, and up-selling with ease and confidence. Rory called him a natural, as the customer who came in for ciabatta rolls ended up walking out with a slice of treacle tart, a raspberry meringue, and a St Clements muffin, or three. Yes, he could sell, and it had been something of a revelation and a quiet source of pride, but it was the quality of the produce that brought the customers back time after time.

Jack mulled over the woman's words. The success of the bakery had taken both him and Rory by surprise, and when the chance of redundancy from his HR Director job had been waved in front of him, Jack had grabbed it with both hands. Instead of pushing himself onto a heaving, sweaty Tube train each morning to spend the day in corporate hell, he and Rory were doing what they had set out to do: working together, laying the foundations of their future. *But it could be an even bigger future with a café tacked on...*

"I can take over now, Jack."

Lance's soft voice, with its West Country burr, jolted Jack from his thoughts. Jack smiled. It was impossible not to. The late teen was tall and gangly, all arms and legs and awkward as though he had yet to grow into his body. He reminded Jack of the foals on his parents' Devonshire estate, and along with the soft accent, it took Jack back to his home before London.

Leaving Lance to look after the shop, Jack made his way into the kitchen, where Mabel pulled a tray of just-cooked muffins from the oven as in the corner, made cooler by the partially open back door, Rory swirled buttercream on top of a batch made earlier.

Concentration held Rory's face still. All the little mannerisms Jack knew so well were nowhere to be seen, tucked away behind his professional concentration. When it came to his culinary creations, Rory was a perfectionist, or at least he was at The Bakehouse. At home, he'd pull out ingredients with abandon, every one of them seemingly unrelated to the other, but every time he produced a masterpiece.

Jack kept quiet. He knew better than to interrupt Rory when he was holding an icing bag and had *that look* on his face. One more muffin and the batch was covered with a final squeeze. Rory stepped back, looked up, and smiled. Jack's heart melted.

"You can help with the finishing touches. Those," Rory said, nodding towards a batch of dark chocolate squares topped with golden caramel buttercream, "are your creation."

"What? The chocolate bruffins?"

"Yup."

The bruffins, as they called them, were the result of a semi-drunken session in the kitchen. A crossover between a brownie and muffin, they were a hundred per cent original as much as they were a hundred per cent delicious. And the buttercream with a hint of salted caramel... well, hadn't that tasted very nice smeared on Rory's—

"Do you want to put the cherry on top?"

"Er... What?"

Rory smiled, the slight narrowing of his eyes and the barely there lift of his lips was all Jack needed to know that Rory was reading every single piece of his mind.

"If you two are going to indulge in innuendo," Mabel said, rolling her eyes, "I'll leave you lads to it."

"I was only asking Jack if he wanted to do things with my cherries."

"I'm more than willing to handle your cherries any day the week, Kincaid." Jack smirked, and plucked the large jar of sour cherries from a nearby shelf.

Rory threw back his head, and laughed. Jack smiled. Rory's reaction, so free and easy, went straight to Jack's heart, suddenly as soft and gooey as the buttercream-topped bruffins.

He hadn't heard much of Rory's laughter over the last few weeks, as the pressure and tension had been turned up not only because of the avalanche of business at The Bakehouse but over their impending wedding, too. It was a sound he needed to hear more of, not just for himself but for Rory's sake, too. Everything that was happening in their lives was supposed to be a celebration, a looking forward, of good things to come. What they weren't supposed to be were stresses and strains. They needed a break, *Rory* needed a break, and Jack knew just what to do to make his man not just smile but laugh long and loud, with his head thrown back.

"Is that the last batch?" Jack asked.

"Yes. This is it for both today and tomorrow, I'm glad to say."

Rory wiped the back of his hand across his brow as if to underline his words. His apron was stained with cake mixes and batters, and he had a smear of icing on his cheek and some on the tip of his nose. Rory was a genius at what he did, but he was bloody messy. It took almost as long to clean the kitchen as it did to prepare and cook the cakes, pastries, and other goodies that flew out of the shop each day.

"Does that mean we don't have to arrive so early tomorrow, boss?" Mabel asked.

Rory thought for a moment, then shook his head. "We've got plenty of stock for the shop for the rest of the day and for tomorrow, but I've got a couple of celebration cakes to bake. All part of a special order."

"But you don't have to cook those first thing, do you? At six in the morning, I mean."

"I suppose not. They can easily be made late-morning as they're not being picked up until the end of the day."

Jack caught Mabel's eye; he could see where this was going, and he kept quiet.

"In that case, I'll open up, with Lance. If there's no baking to be done first thing, it means you can have a later start. You're looking knackered, boss." Mabel added, her voice softer.

"I don't know..."

"Well, I do." Jack put down the jar of sour cherries he still held. "Mabel and Lance have opened up for us before."

Mabel snorted. "Opened up for you? Me and Lance ran this place for a whole week back in the spring. We didn't burn it down, we didn't break into the safe, we didn't eat all the stock, and we didn't punch one customer. Not one. I'd call that a result, wouldn't you?"

Jack swallowed a laugh.

"W-*ell*..." Rory said.

Rory was at the tipping point. Jack could see the indecision in his dark brown eyes. When it came to The Bakehouse, he needed to feel in control, to be on hand to steer the bakery along its smooth course, but he couldn't disguise his desire for a long lie-in and breakfast in bed. He just needed a little push to make the right decision.

"An evening out. Dinner at Caravaggio's, a nightcap at Lucille's Jazz and Blues, and a lazy breakfast brought to you in bed on a tray by me, with a rose between my teeth. How can you resist?"

Mabel gagged, loud and dramatic.

"Jack, you don't need to let all of our secrets escape. It's not between your teeth that you hold the rose."

Rory was laughing, his eyes bright and shining. His face had lost the tension that had seemed to hold every muscle tight. *This* was the man Jack had been missing, and this was the man he wanted back. Even if it was only for one evening and a long and leisurely morning. But Rory needed that one final push.

"And don't forget, Mabel is a trained pastry chef."

Mabel nodded, slow and sage-like.

"I am indeed, and *he*," she said, nodding towards Rory, "needs to be reminded of that from time to time.

I can do a lot more to help in this place, and I'm willing to do it."

It was all Rory needed.

"Well, if you're sure...?"

"Piece of cake." Mabel grinned at her own pun.

"That's settled, then," Jack said as he unscrewed the jar of cherries, and retrieved a pair of tongs from a large container of utensils on the side. "For the moment, I'm on cherry duty." Jack fished out his keys from his jeans pocket and threw them over to Mabel, who caught them with ease in one hand. "But after that, we're off for the day. Agreed?"

Rory nodded and smiled, and Jack smiled back.

CHAPTER FOUR

Jack put the breakfast-laden tray on the bedside cabinet and plucked the phone from Rory's hands.

"Mabel knows what she's doing."

"I just wanted to—"

"Check on everything, be there when you're *not actually* there. Didn't we say we were going to have some time out, even if was just a few hours?"

Rory's lips twisted up in a sheepish smile. "Yes, we did, but I just find it hard to let go."

Jack didn't say anything as he retrieved the tray and settled down back in bed with Rory. They were going to have a morning doing exactly as he said they would. A long and lazy breakfast in bed. No checking phones, no talking about the bakery, and definitely no discussion about the wedding. Just him and Rory, the rest of the world and all its stresses and strains left outside the door.

The wedding. Jack smothered his sigh. It was worrying Rory to pieces. The strained lines on Rory's face, the lower lip clenched between his teeth, the tight smile when Diana called and they switched to speakerphone, allowing her clear and confident tones to ring out. All of it told its own story.

His mother had taken over the organisation with military precision, just as he knew she would. He'd thought it a good thing, knowing the most important day in his and Rory's life was in expert hands.

Diana's enthusiastic takeover of the arrangements was supposed to ease the stress, not add to it. She was a born organiser, it was almost part of her DNA, and she'd swung into action, intent in her quest to create a true De Lacy wedding. On a small scale, they'd been insistent on that. But perhaps it being a *De Lacy* wedding was part of the problem. It wasn't just a De Lacy wedding, it was a *Kincaid* wedding, too. And he'd reminded her of that, no, he had *stressed* that, the last time he and Rory were at the Manor House. Just the pair of them, over an early morning cup of tea in the big kitchen. Jack chewed on his bacon, too preoccupied to appreciate its salty, savoury juiciness.

"... get this bacon from? Jack?"

"Hmm? What's that? Oh, er, the new butchers."

Jack mentioned the name of the high-end independent that had opened locally.

"It's a great breakfast."

Rory's smile, and his eyes, were bright and clear. Their evening out, and now the treat of a full English when normally it was a grabbed coffee and a hastily eaten slice of toast before plunging headfirst into the day had done Rory a power of good Jack's troublesome thoughts broke up and drifted away like clouds in the face of Rory's warm, sunny smile.

They finished their plates of piled-high bacon, eggs, sausage and mushrooms with a satisfied sigh.

"Those croissants look good."

"These?" Jack said, plucking up one of the icing sugar-dusted almond pastries. He broke a piece off and lifted it to Rory's lips.

"They're not bad. I know the baker."

"Just *not bad*?" Rory quirked a brow, laughing as he pulled the piece from Jack's fingers with his teeth.

"Mmmm, delicious. This baker you know is a talented boy."

"Oh yes, he's that all right." Jack's lips lifted in a sly smile. "He's a very, very talented boy."

Jack's dick twitched in agreement.

"Yeah? What's so talented about him?"

Rory's words sent a shiver down Jack's backbone. His fiancé's words were low and rough edged, and Jack swore Rory's breathing was faster and shallower than moments before. Jack dumped the tray on the floor, what was left of their breakfast forgotten about.

"But he's not the only one." Jack ran a hand across Rory's stomach, smiling as Rory's muscles twitched beneath his touch, before brushing the length of his hot, hard cock. Jack swept his thumb pad across the edge of the crown and was rewarded with Rory's shuddering groan.

"I know his boyfriend, too," Jack breathed, "and he's just as talented in his own way."

"Yeah?"

Rory's breathy question exploded a burst of heat in Jack's groin. His dick twitched, hungry for more than breakfast.

He lurched towards the bedside cabinet, ready to rummage for the lube they kept in the drawer. But Rory was ahead of him, already holding up the large, well-used tube. Jack grabbed it from his fiancé's hand, their eyes meeting. Rory's smile was wicked, the deep brown of his eyes turned black with want. This was what Rory needed, this is what *he* needed, just the two of them turning on that relief valve, releasing all the pressure.

Jack grabbed a pillow and rammed it beneath Rory's hips, tilting him up. A slick of lube, and Rory's gasp as the cool gel smeared his heated skin. Jack's insistent fingers circled the tight muscle, and Rory shifted, pulling his legs up higher, wider, giving Jack the access he needed. Jack's heart thundered as his own cock bobbed against his stomach, demanding attention. But what he needed would have to wait because this, here, now, was all about the man with the demanding eyes, the flushed face, and the deep red lips, damp and partially open as fast, ragged breaths pushed their way past.

Rory gasped as Jack pushed in first one finger, then a second. A trembling sigh reverberated through Rory's body.

"You like that, Ro? You like feeling me inside you?" Jack whispered. He smiled as Rory swallowed and attempted to answer, his words dragged back by another gasp as he nodded hard and clenched his eyes closed.

Oh yes... He knew what his fiancé liked.

Jack knew where to touch, where to lick, where to suck, and where to stroke. He eased his fingers deeper, flexing against the tight, hot channel, his own dick on fire, and aching as pre-cum pooled at the slit. His dick jerked, and his balls tightened as Rory's muscles clenched hard against his deepening fingers. Rory gasped out a strangled moan, his hips snapping upwards as Jack found and stroked his gland. Jack smiled, and stroked some more.

"Oh fuck, Jack. Fucking *hell*."

Rory's eyes flew open. The brown of his irises had been devoured by his pupils. His face flushed red, and his lips were wet and pillowy. Raven black hair stuck to his sweaty brow as his eyes bored into Jack's, full of need, desire, and want.

"Jack, I—I need... ahhh," Rory stammered as Jack rubbed at his gland.

"What is it you need, babe? Tell me what you need..." Jack's words played and teased Rory as much as his fingers. He knew exactly what his man needed, but Rory was going to have to ask. A third finger joined the first two, and Jack massaged deeper, flexing, stroking, and flexing again.

"Are you going to make me beg?"

"Oh yeah." Jack grinned. His man was *so good* at begging.

"You know what I want, *please*..." Rory's voice faded into a needy whine.

"Do I? Is it this you want?" Jack pushed harder against Rory's sweet spot. "Or this?" He pressed his lips to Rory's chest, sucking hard on a raised pink nipple.

Rory's moan filled the room.

"You bastard, you..." The rest of Rory's words dissolved into a breathy groan as Jack's fingers sped up, working Rory harder and faster.

Jack eased his fingers free. He could read Rory's body and its wants and desires like a large print book. Rory was near the edge, but Jack wasn't going to let him tumble over it yet. He pressed down on the base of Rory's throbbing, swollen cock, his mouth watering as a gossamer-thin trail of pre-cum stretched between Rory's wet slit and his stomach. But Rory wasn't the only once close to the edge. Jack's own need was searing and white-hot, his desperation to bury himself deep inside his lover so intense his breath was snatched away as every muscle in his body trembled.

Blindly, Jack fumbled for the lube, discarded somewhere on the bed. With shaking hands, he squeezed some into his palm, slathering it along the length of his dick. He winced, and sucked in a sharp breath as his fingers swept against the engorged head; so tender and nervy, the slightest brush was delicious anguish.

Rory widened and raised his legs. Hooking his arms under Rory's flexed knees, Jack brought his fiancé's legs up and over his shoulders. He gazed down at the man beneath him. Rory was exposed and open, physically and emotionally. But it wasn't just the want and desire Jack saw in the depths of Rory's dark eyes. It was something deeper, stronger, and heart-wrenching in its honesty.

He saw trust, and the unshakeable knowledge

shining out at him that Jack would never, ever hurt him.

Jack swallowed. The belief Rory was placing in him was almost too much to bear. But this was how it was between them, this was who they were. Sex, making love, was way beyond the physical. It had gone way, way beyond that. It was a giving, not just of their bodies but of their hearts and souls too.

"Jack."

His name, whispered on the softest breath, was an explosion in his head and in his heart.

"I love you, Ro. I love you more than everything. I don't—"

"No talk, not now, just... ahhh, fuck, Jack, *yes*."

Already lined up, Jack thrust his hips forward, pushing deep. It was everything they not just wanted but craved, to release the pressure that was building up and up around them.

With every push of his hips, Jack was met with Rory's own. As Jack drove into him, Rory thrust back. The slap of flesh on flesh was harsh and loud, and matched only by their ragged, desperate breaths. Lips crashed against lips as hungry mouths drank from each other's. The bed rocked, the wooden headboard banging into the wall as the frame creaked and groaned under the onslaught of their burning, sweat-slicked bodies.

Jack buried his face in the crook of Rory's neck. He inhaled as deep as he could, then deeper still, desperate to fill his senses with the scent of Rory's arousal. The salty tang of sweat combined with the musk of sex. Jack breathed in harder, every muscle shuddering and out of control. He picked up his rhythm, forcing the pace, pushing in deeper, so deep it was as though he was merging with and melding into Rory's body. He licked and sucked on the thin skin on the edge of Rory's collarbone, licking faster and sucking harder, drawing the flesh into his mouth, feeling it warm, wet, and pliant. He clamped down with his teeth. Rory shuddered beneath him. He would be marked. There would be bruises, dark evidence imprinted on his lover's skin, the badge of what they had shared.

Mine, all mine. The stark, hard words came from some primitive and shadowy place deep within Jack. Possession, he craved possession. He sucked harder, his lips clamped hard to Rory's skin, his chest thrilling, his hips pumping harder as Rory whimpered and shuddered beneath him. Fingers, hard and clawing, shot through his hair, scratching at his scalp. Pain shimmered across the thin skin, and Jack welcomed it, welcomed the hard and visceral response from his lover.

Rory's fingers tangled through his hair, tearing at the fine strands and speeding a spasm of tingling pain the length of Jack's backbone. Jack bit and sucked deeper on Rory's bruised flesh as his scalp burned from Rory's twisting, clutching, clawing fingers, buried in his hair. Rory groaned incomprehensible words which could have been curses, pleas, or both.

Beneath Jack, Rory's muscles twitched and spasmed. Rory was close, so close to the edge. Jack felt it in the pulsing of his muscles, in the hitching of his breath and in his name, gasped out from a sex-roughened throat. Jack grasped the hot flesh of Rory's swollen shaft. A flick of his thumb pad across the weeping head was all it took.

A shuddering, broken groan and a final snap of his hips, and Rory emptied himself, warm and wet, into Jack's hand. The salt-laden cum drenched Jack's senses. He pulled his hand free from Rory's softening cock and licked his soaking fingers, tasting the very essence of the man who lay wet and panting beneath him. The taste on Jack's lips and tongue, of his fiancé, of his lover, of his man.

Of Rory.

Jack's heart, beating wild and out of control, stuttered and shuddered at the same time his balls pulled up and tightened into hard pebbles, and he cried out as his dick pumped warm and sticky wetness deep into Rory's body.

Jack lay panting, fighting for breath as his lungs

burned. Sweat plastered his hair to his forehead and beaded down his temples and cheeks. Cum coated them both, sticking them together on the rumpled and drenched sheets. His breath slowed and levelled out, and the white noise that filled his head faded to nothing. Rory's legs had slipped from his shoulders and lay coiled around his thighs. Fingers that had clutched and scratched now trailed their way down his back, along the valley of his spine.

Raising himself up onto unsteady elbows, Jack gazed down into Rory's face, calm and relaxed and with no trace of the tension that lately was holding him tight every hour, minute, and second of the day. That alone was worth more than Jack could put into words; he shifted, and swept a lock of damp hair away from Rory's brow. Gentle, dark chocolate-brown eyes gazed up at him. A smile, soft and almost shy, lifted the edges of his lips.

"I think you should bring me breakfast in bed every morning," Rory said.

Jack chuckled as he rolled over onto his back and turned his head to look at Rory besides him.

"I don't think I have the energy to do that."

"Well, perhaps you need to ensure you keep your energy levels high. You never know when they'll be called upon."

Rory nudged him, urging him to sit up. With a

grumble, Jack pushed himself up, on arms that were still shaking, and settled back against the headboard.

Rory bent over the side of the bed, re-emerging with their abandoned breakfast, and Jack's stomach rumbled as Rory settled the tray with the croissants and coffee besides them on the bed. The croissants were no longer fresh from the oven, and the coffee was barely lukewarm. It was the most tempting meal Jack had ever been presented with.

"Hard, cold croissants and tepid coffee." Rory tucked in. "It's just as well our customers can't see us now," he said between greedy mouthfuls.

Jack snorted. "I'd be bloody worried if they could."

Rory smiled but said nothing as they made short work of the cold remains of their breakfast.

They lay back, and Jack carded his fingers through Rory's damp hair.

"I don't want you worrying or stressing out, okay?" Jack didn't need to spell out what he was talking about.

Rory hesitated before he nodded, and Jack suppressed the groan. Why had he said anything? They were supposed to be revelling in a post-coital glow. Rory had needed the knot of tension to be loosened, yet there *he* was, pulling it tight once more. The light-as-air croissants sat heavy in Jack's stomach, and the cold coffee was bitter and acidic.

"Hey."

Long and slender fingers trailed down his cheek and along his jawbone before sweeping across his lower lip.

"I kind of think it would be more worrying if I wasn't getting stressed out. Running a new business and getting married to a hot bit of posh isn't something a boy does every day."

Jack quirked his brow. "A bit of posh? Is that how you see me?"

"Of course. Because that's what you are, aren't you?"

Jack narrowed his eyes, giving Rory his best mock glare. If he was trying to look fierce or offended, it didn't work, because Rory started to laugh as he put the tray back on the floor and then snuggled into Jack's side.

"I think everybody should have a bit of posh in their lives," he said as he nuzzled into Jack, "but this particular example is well and truly mine."

Nobody else's, only Rory's... the thought was sweet and his smile soft. Jack closed his eyes and wrapped Rory up in his arms as he drifted off into the waiting embrace of sleep.

CHAPTER FIVE

Rory stirred the rich beef casserole before tasting a little and deciding it needed more seasoning. With the garlic and rosemary ciabatta and mince pies he'd brought back from the bakery, it was a good meal in the face of the freezing cold weather that had descended in the last couple of days.

Hours and hours before, at 5:00 am, when sunrise had still been a vague thought, he'd thrown the meat, vegetables, and stock into the slow cooker when Jack had hardly been stirring in the warmth of their bed. Rory didn't resent that Jack woke and started later; it gave him the quiet time he craved and needed, to gather together his thoughts about the day ahead. Today, though, thoughts about all things sweet laced with warm seasonal spice had been joined by those of

Diana, joining them for dinner and which would be full of wedding talk.

"Stop bitching," he murmured to himself.

Details mattered, he knew they did. Lack of attention to detail could foil the best-laid plans. Hadn't his lack of attention, in the first weeks of the bakery, resulted in a whole batch of burned-to-a-cinder gingerbread? It had been fit only for the bin. He glanced at his watch; almost 7:30 in the evening. He had barely had time to breathe during the day, and was tired down to his bones.

When Diana had called earlier in the day to check what time she was expected, he'd been in the middle of packing up yet another private order of mixed muffins and cupcakes, at the same time thinking about the icing challenge he had ahead of him for a christening cake as he tweaked a recipe for a spiced latte cheesecake. He'd heard something about ribbons, or he thought it was ribbons; he'd snapped back at her and immediately felt shitty as the silence yawned down the phone. His stumbling apology had been met with unerring politeness, which had made him feel even worse.

His wedding. God, he wanted to marry Jack so badly. They should have gone, quietly and without fuss, to the local register office, emerging with identical rings wrapped proudly around their ring fingers... He stopped stirring. Jack would have done it if he'd asked. Rory had no doubt of that at all.

"But could I have asked?" Rory said aloud into the silent kitchen, staring into the bubbling, dark depths of the casserole. No, never. It would have wounded Jack to the bone, as though their wedding were something to be hidden away. Jack would have agreed, because his happiness was Jack's, but Rory would have seen the light go out in his man's eyes, and he could never, ever let that happen.

The slam of the front door and the sound of two voices threw Rory out of his unsettling thoughts. He put the lid back on the casserole and went into the living room.

"Rory." Diana took him in a light hug and placed a kiss on his cheek.

Tall, slim, and elegant, Diana was dressed in her signature light blue cashmere. Her Chanel No. 5 perfume filled the room and made Rory's nose twitch, overpowering even the aroma of the herby casserole.

"You look tired, my dear," Diana said as she studied him through clear blue eyes, eyes that were the exact shade of Jack's.

"We're really busy at the bakery.' Jack answered his mother, but he looked at Rory, his face lit up in a bright smile. Rory returned his smile at the same time he swept away some melting snowflakes from Jack's hair.

"Perhaps you should employ more staff." Diana held out her green waxed coat for Jack to take; he disappeared to hang it on the stand in the hallway.

A spark of irritation flared in Rory's chest. Yes, they would need to seriously consider taking on additional staff if the bakery continued to be as busy as it was. But successful as they were, it was still a new business, and he and Jack had agreed they needed to be prudent during their first year of operation. Diana was a savvy businesswoman, as was Roger, so the blasé suggestion that they *should employ more staff* was out of place.

I'm tired, that's all it is... "It's something to think about in the New Year. Let me get you a cup of tea."

"I think wine would be a better suggestion," Jack said as he came back into the living room. "I've got some of the Piaf Estate merlot. Dad gave me a case the last time I was down at the Manor." Jack threw the words over his shoulder as he went to the spare room, where the wine that cost almost a hundred pounds per bottle was stored in a cool cupboard.

"Running your own business is exhausting, isn't it? It doesn't matter how organised you believe yourself to be, there are never enough hours in the day or days in the week." Diana's smile was rueful, sympathetic, and understanding all at once.

Rory sank down into the chair opposite her, and the tension in his shoulders and stiff neck relaxed a little. Between them, Diana and Roger ran a huge, thriving estate. Hundreds, either directly or indirectly, relied on its success for their livelihood. He just had the one shop...

"It is. I was prepared for all the hard work, it was never something I was afraid of." Rory shrugged. He'd worked in enough restaurants after he'd gained his catering qualification, working his way up from the bottom rung. The food industry, whether it was working at the bottom of the pecking order in a busy kitchen, or running one's own business, was tough mentally and physically. "But when it's your own..."

Diana bent forward and laid her elegant long-fingered hand on his knee, and gave him a brief squeeze in understanding.

"The first year is always the hardest. It's when you put in all the groundwork. But you have a very good, solid, and successful business there. Both you and Jack should be very proud of what you've achieved."

"I am proud, but I can't deny it's been exhausting, and what with the wedding—"

"Which is why I wanted to take that stress away from you and Jack," Diana said, removing her hand

and settling back into the sofa. "A wedding, even a small and simple one takes a lot of planning."

The muscles that had relaxed in Rory's neck and shoulders knotted up once more. Simple? It had gone way beyond what his definition of simple was.

Rory had only been to one wedding. A bland modern church, with a baby screaming at the back the parents hadn't thought to take out. It had been followed by a free bar in the function room of the local pub, with a brown buffet of sausage rolls, quiche, and ham or cheese sandwiches with bowls of crisps dotted around. It had been horrible, and nothing like he wanted his and Jack's wedding to be, but... he licked his lips and leant forward.

"Diana, I, we—"

"That casserole smells divine, Ro." Jack came back in, carrying the wine and three glasses.

"It certainly does." Diana smiled. "The hotel will have to do very well indeed to surpass your culinary skills."

Rory nodded as he took a sip of the wine Jack poured. He knew it was out of this world, but he couldn't taste a thing.

"Numbers have now been formally confirmed, and we have a wedding party of forty-five."

"Forty-five?" Rory blurted out.

Who the hell were these forty-five? He and Jack,

Jack's immediate family, and a handful of friends didn't make *forty-five* wedding guests. Whoever these extra people were, he didn't know them, and he didn't want them coming to his wedding. He put his wine glass down on the coffee table with more force than he had meant to, almost sloshing some over the rim. He opened his mouth to ask Diana to explain about the *forty-five*, but Jack got in first.

"Forty-five guests? Mum, there's no way the list we drew up — and agreed to — came to forty-five. Where have these extra people come from?"

Rory's eyes flitted between Jack and Diana. Jack was frowning, his brows pulled into a tight V. Diana was as controlled as ever.

"Aunt Amelia phoned in something of a panic last week. Boris and his family have arrived back in the UK, somewhat unexpectedly. He was most upset they had not received an invitation."

"Boris? But he's in the middle of the rain forest in South America. Or was."

Boris? Who the fuck is Boris? Rory looked at Jack, lifting his brows in question. It was Diana who answered.

"Boris is Jack's cousin. He and Jack were good friends as children and teenagers. After university, he went to Brazil to study rare fungi and stayed."

Fungi. The only fungi Rory was interested in were

those which he cooked with butter and garlic, and a splash or two of wine.

Diana shrugged. "I'm sorry. I should have told you both, but I rather wanted to keep him as a surprise. And now I find I have surprised you, but not in the way I'd hoped."

"You should have told us, Mum. It'll be good to see him again, but Boris and his family don't make up the forty-five. Do they?"

"No, the additional guests are estate workers. Eight, in total. Your father and I have arranged transport and overnight accommodation for those who have worked loyally and tirelessly for the family for years, and who are now mainly retired. It's tradition to extend invites to those who have helped make the estate the success it is. You know that, Jack."

"Yes — if we were getting married in the village or even the county, I'd get that. But we're not." Jack's frown deepened.

"Erm..."

Two sets of eyes locked onto Rory.

"The estate workers. I, erm, I'm fine with that. I think it's a nice thing to do. But you should have told us, Diana. Jack?" He turned to Jack, who shrugged his shoulders, but his frown had lessened.

"Yes, okay." Jack huffed. "As long as it is only eight. But you should have consulted us, not informed us after the fact. We would have okayed it," he said, flashing a quick glance at Rory, who answered with a tiny nod. "But that's not the point. It's our day, Mum, mine and Rory's. Don't forget that."

Diana inclined her head. They sipped at their wine, the only sound in the room the crackling wood burning stove.

The tension in Rory's shoulders lessened as Jack's hand settled between his shoulder blades. He looked at Jack. *Are you really okay with this?* his fiancé's eyes seemed to ask. Rory smiled his answer. It was a good thing of Diana and Roger to do. Rory had come to know his future in-laws enough to know they would have felt a commitment to holding up the tradition... *but they bloody well should have said something first...*

The timer on the oven pinged, piercing the awkward silence. Rory jumped up and raced for the kitchen.

He let out a long breath as he pulled the bread, spiked with rosemary, from the oven.

"Ro?"

Jack came up behind him, and Rory sighed as he leant backwards and let Jack take his weight.

"Sorry about that. So, we now have the absentee cousin and his wife and three kids. But you'll like Boris, I promise."

"Don't forget the estate workers. It's a, a generous thing to do, and I don't mind that. Honestly."

"Really?"

Rory nodded. "Really," he said, as he turned in Jack's arms and snuggled into him. "I don't mind about your cousin, or people who have worked for the estate for donkeys' years."

"I can hear a but."

Rory huffed out a small laugh. Jack knew him too well.

"It's the rest of it that sends my stress levels soaring. The hotel, it's fabulous, I know it is, but it wasn't what we wanted—"

"Our first choice couldn't accommodate us, you know that."

"I know, I get it... But announcements in The Times and in those huntin', shootin', fishin' magazines your parents have—"

Jack sniggered. "Yes, I know. They don't even hunt or shoot. They do fish, though. Perhaps a discreet announcement in Salmon Monthly or Carp News would have been more appropriate."

"Oh, stop it." Rory gave Jack a shove, but he couldn't help smiling. "But bespoke suits? I looked up how much that's all costing. It's too much, Jack." *Enough to place a deposit down on a house in the town I grew up in...*

"If you can't wear handmade tailoring on your wedding day, when can you? My parents are paying for our tailoring, just like they're paying for George's suit, and Caroline's dressmaking bill. They're doing it because they want to, Ro. And yes, I know they're shouldering the bulk of the cost of the wedding, but it's their gift to us, a gift they *want* to give. This was all agreed, right at the start."

"Oh, I know. I know, I know, I know..." He did, he really did, but...

"It's still going to be our day, and that's what you have to focus on."

"You make it all sound so reasonable," Rory grumbled.

And maybe it was reasonable. In the world Jack had grown up in, smart weddings in plush West End hotels *were* reasonable, so were bespoke suits, so were page boys and flower girls... at least he'd put his foot down about *those*.

"I'm sorry. I should be more appreciative of what your parents are doing for us," Rory mumbled into Jack's chest.

"It's not about being sorry, and it's certainly not about being appreciative or thinking you can't have a say. Remember the pageboys? Hmm? You were a braver man than I, going up against my mother over the Monsters not being dressed up in velvet and lace.

Urggh, what a thought." Jack gave an exaggerated shudder, and Rory laughed. "Honestly, Ro, it's going to be fine. More than fine. It's going to be the most wonderful day, one we'll remember for all the right reasons for the rest of our lives. I want us, *you*, to not just to enjoy but to revel in it because we're only getting married once. Okay?"

CHAPTER SIX

The last-minute wedding preparations consisted of flower arrangements for the tables and place settings, before the conversation glided seamlessly onto recent events in Polton Lacy.

After three large glasses of merlot, Rory's tensions had smoothed over, and as he listened, he floated on a semi-drunken cloud. It was nice, he decided, and it was where he wanted to stay for as long as he could. Flower arrangements and place settings, what was there to discuss about *flower arrangements* and *place settings?* Last-minute plans to sign off, Diana had said.

"We had the Christmas fête last weekend." Diana took a delicate sip of wine.

"Is it like the Easter fête, only at Christmas?" Rory asked as he gulped down a mouthful.

Diana nodded. "Essentially, it is. Lots of stalls

selling seasonal produce and Christmas food and drink. It all takes place in the lower field, and in the early evening we have a special service in St Peter's. It's my favourite event in the village calendar. It was such a shame you couldn't be there."

"Caroline telephoned earlier in the week," Jack said, referring to his sister. "She said something about there being an incident during the service, but she had to ring off because the Monsters were playing up."

When aren't they? Rory took another slug of wine, emptying his glass with a smack of his lips. The merlot was a lot better than the red they normally picked up from the supermarket. About ninety pounds' worth better.

"I'll open up another bottle, shall I?" Rory pushed himself up from the table before either Jack or Diana could answer.

Dinner was the first thing he'd eaten since before six that morning, when he had scarfed down a croissant from the bakery, and the first glass had hit his empty stomach. He knew he was well on the way to getting drunk, and in a little unfocused corner of his brain, he knew opening up a second bottle wasn't the best idea...

Fuck it. It was Saturday night, which meant no work tomorrow. If he ended up with a headache in the morning, it would be worth it for the merlot cloud he was floating on. The cork came out with a satisfying pop.

"...Desmond made rather a mess of things, but it was not his fault. The vicar's wife was most unhappy about having a donkey in the church and made her views very clear. As I did mine." Diana huffed. "The dreadful woman wouldn't, or couldn't, understand that it's a Polton Lacy tradition. She upset not only Desmond but the young shepherds, too, none of whom was older than five. Really, I think she needs to take much of the blame for what happened."

"What? Donkeys?" Rory plonked the open bottle of wine in the middle of the table and looked between Diana and Jack. He'd only been away from the table for a couple or so minutes, and they were talking about — donkeys.

"Mum's just telling me about the service after the Christmas fête," Jack said with a grin.

"Desmond is a super little donkey. Simply super." Diana turned to Rory. "He's normally such a gentle and docile little chap, but something set him off, and it was, with no doubt in my mind, the vicar's ghastly wife. He not only relieved himself, in a very spectacular manner, but he then scampered the length of the nave and barrelled into the vicar, knocking the silly man over. He quite destroyed the manger and nativity scene, which the Polton Lacy Ladies' Guild have been the custodians of for almost one hundred years. The vicar, that is, not Desmond."

Rory glanced over at Jack, who was hiding his barely concealed laughter behind his wine glass.

"So, this donkey," Jack said. "He—"

"Desmond. His character is unimpeachable. He was quite the star attraction at the harvest festival," Diana added.

"So Desmond effectively wrecked the service and the church? I expect the good ladies of the Guild were distraught."

Rory met Jack's eye, and they grinned at each other.

Rory took another slurp from his topped-up glass. A running amock donkey that had managed to shit everywhere, a destroyed nativity scene, and the vicar assaulted, even if it was just by a *super little donkey* called Desmond. He threw another glance at Jack, who had given up trying to hide his laughter if the shaking of his shoulders was anything to go by.

Rory guzzled some more wine. *Wonder if there are any photos or vids on the internet...* He'd have a look, later. *Hashtag DesmondTheDonkey...*

"Jack. When you have quite finished laughing, you should remember the Christmas service is a highlight of the village's year. The donkey is most important. He is central to the occasion, the star attraction without a doubt. We are very careful in choosing who should have the honour of bearing The Virgin and the baby Jesus. Several donkeys were considered, including entrants from Dell's Donkey World, but this year there really was no competition; it had to be Desmond from Devonshire Donkeyarium."

"The—what?" Rory's hand, halfway to his mouth and clutching his glass, froze. Had he heard right? Maybe he was more drunk than he realised.

"The Devonshire Donkeyarium. It's a centre dedicated to all things donkey related. It really is a very worthy charity. They take donkeys to old people's homes, for the elderly to stroke and pet. It does the old things a power of good. The elderly residents, I mean, not the donkeys. Anyway," Diana said as she patted the corners of her mouth with her napkin, "the vicar sustained a fractured tibia, the flower display which the ladies of The Friends of St Peter's had spent many hours arranging were trampled beneath Desmond's hooves, and the little baby Jesus, which is actually an old china doll with only one remaining eye, had its head severed from its neck in all the mayhem. It gave the verger quite a fright as it rolled towards him. He had to be revived with smelling salts."

Rory blinked. Mayhem at the village church. *Bloody brilliant.*

"Fortunately, the child who had the honour to play

the Virgin Mary and who'd been thrown from poor Desmond's back when he reared up in distress, was unharmed but quite distraught. The chairman of the Donkeyarium, Colonel Huffington, rose to the occasion and soothed the ruffled feathers of the child's parents by offering a family pass valid for one year to the Donkeyarium, along with a complimentary cream tea at their café on their first visit. Not that the cream tea should mollify them." Diana sniffed. "Their cream tea really is quite a travesty. Supermarket scones, clotted cream if it can even be called that as it's imported from Bulgaria, and budget-range strawberry jam. I understand they wish to spend as much as they can on the care and welfare of the donkeys, but really. Devonshire is the home of the cream tea. They really should be duty-bound to provide the best example they can."

"Yes, I suppose they should," Rory said, blinking hard.

"Next year, we will have to reassess how we handle the service. Thankfully, Desmond was unharmed during the fracas, and that really is the main thing." Diana dropped her napkin onto her empty plate.

"But the vicar," Jack said, "was he okay?"

Rory glanced at Jack. Didn't he know the vicar was way below Desmond in Diana's pecking order?

"Oh yes," Diana said, airily waving her hand. "He

was treated at the cottage hospital, where he also received a tetanus jab."

"For a fractured tibia thingy?" Rory said. "You don't need a jab for that."

Diana shrugged. "Unfortunately, in the mêlée, the vicar also received a bite to his posterior."

"You mean he got bitten on the arse?" Jack was convulsed with laughter. "Who did that? The donkey?"

"Don't be ridiculous, Jack." Diana frowned. "Of course Desmond didn't bite the vicar. Do you think the Donkeyarium or indeed the chair of the Nativity Committee, who happens to be me, would allow a savage donkey anywhere near children? No. The silly man fell rather heavily against Badger, who had a very important role as one of the Shepherds' flock." She stared at Jack, her face straight.

"So you had a golden labrador pretending to be a sheep?" Rory said. Perhaps they had dressed Badger up in a woolly jumper so he could get better into the role. Method acting for dogs, maybe.

Badger. A warm glow came over Rory that wasn't only from the merlot. The golden lab had been his near-constant companion during his first fateful visit to Jack's family home. *If only we had a garden...* He'd love to have Badger with him and Jack in London, but all the while they lived in the flat it would remain nothing more than an impossible dream.

"Yes, of course we did," Diana replied as if it were the most natural thing in the world. "Bruno was also taking part," she added, referring to her husband's big and lumbering old dog. "We also had Mr. Giles' sheepdog, Tess."

Rory had no idea who Mr. Giles was, and neither did Jack if the slight raise of his shoulders was any indication.

"Surely you don't think we would take *sheep* into the church?"

Didn't stop you taking the fucking mad donkey though, did it? Maybe it was best if he kept that thought to himself.

"The silly man made such a terrible fuss." Diana's frown deepened. "I took it as something of a personal insult that he thought he could catch something from Badger."

"But a dog bite, Mum..." Jack shrugged.

"As long as Badger was all right." Rory topped up his glass.

"Exactly." Diana's frown turned into a smile. "I inspected Badger myself, and he was quite unharmed. He's a very good and placid dog and he only reacted like he did due to extreme provocation. I am happy to say the curate was able to step in for the vicar and once the nave was cleaned up and order restored, the service came to a satisfactory end — and was followed by the customary Christmas tea in the village hall."

Rory escaped to the kitchen, where he dumped their plates on the side by the sink. He pulled the mince pies from the oven, set on low, and dug the pot of clotted cream from the fridge. He scanned the label. Not from Bulgaria, thank God.

"That village and everything that goes on there gets more bizarre with every passing year. And that's coming from somebody who was born and brought up there."

Rory smiled as Jack came in and slid his arms around his waist.

"Mmm. That's nice." Rory twisted around in Jack's arms. "Promise me something?"

"Anything."

"Please don't greet me on our wedding day on the back of a donkey, even if it is Donkeyarium Desmond."

"But we have to have animals. It's De Lacy tradition."

"What?" Rory stared up into Jack's deadpan face, but the twinkling in Jack's eyes gave him away. Rory thumped him on the chest. "Don't frighten me like that, Jack, because knowing your family and animals..."

Jack laughed. "No donkeys, I promise you. You seem more relaxed than earlier. Are you?"

"Yes, with a little help from Mr. Merlot."

Jack narrowed his eyes. "I think Mr. Merlot has done a very admirable job, but maybe some coffee with dessert?"

"Don't get any more pissed, you mean?" *Too late for that.*

Another glass would have gone down well, but Jack was right. Getting plastered in front of his soon-to-be mother-in-law wasn't perhaps his best call. "You go through. I'll bring all this in, and the coffee too."

CHAPTER SEVEN

Jack stretched, yawned, and smiled as the warm body wrapped around him tightened its grip.

"Hey," Jack said as he shifted round to face Rory. "How are you feeling this morning?"

Rory opened one eye, but it seemed like too much effort as he let it drop closed.

"I'm fine. Two large coffees and a pint of water before going to bed have made sure of that. I think."

Rory peeled his eyes open and smiled up at Jack. They were a little red, but other than that, there was no sign he was too much the worse for wear from an evening with Mr. Merlot.

"Mmm, Sunday," Rory murmured as he snuggled in closer to Jack.

Jack knew exactly what Rory meant. It was the one

day of the week The Bakehouse was closed. It didn't mean they didn't work, as they would often go in on Sunday evenings to prepare for the week ahead. But today was different.

Jack had had a quiet word with Mabel and Lance. The Bakehouse had its firm favourites that were guaranteed to sell, but they also had a rotating list of 'Specials'. To keep the offer fresh, Rory said. It made good business sense, as it brought customers back. Later today, Mabel and Lance would go to the shop to prepare the half-dozen 'Specials' to be baked, or prepped to be baked, first thing on Monday morning, alongside the regular offer.

Mabel had been more than happy to help out, as was Lance, who'd slipped into the role of apprentice baker. He and Rory were lucky to have the two of them working for them, and Jack made a mental note to ensure they both received a healthy bonus in their next pay, plus a half day off in lieu of going in that evening. So he and Rory had a full day together, with no demands on their time. It was a luxury they seldom had anymore, and Jack was determined to make the day all about his fiancé.

"What do you want to do today, Ro?"

Rory's answer was to snuggle closer, bumping Jack with his half-hard dick. Rory may still have been half-asleep, but he obviously had his own ideas about how they should start the day.

"Oh, I can think of a thing or two." Rory scraped his teeth along the side of Jack's neck.

Jack shivered. Rory got him every time, in that tiny little space below his earlobe. Sometimes, Jack thought that little patch of skin, no bigger than his thumb pad, was the most sensitive part of his body. Until Rory wrapped his hand around his cock and swept his finger over his slit. Then, that was the most sensitive. Or perhaps it was—

Jack released a jagged sigh as Rory kissed his way down his body. His cock was awake and sitting up, ready and eager to greet the day. He inhaled a long and shaky breath as Rory nuzzled into his groin, making what was already warm, hot. Jack flopped his legs open wide, giving Rory the access his insistent mouth was demanding.

"Ah, fuck." Jack breathed out a trembling breath as Rory licked a wide stripe from the base of his dick all the way up.

A warm hand captured his balls and gently massaged as the tip of one finger brushed across the tender, nervy skin of his perineum. Jack's breath hitched. The touch was feather-light, but it'd sent his senses into orbit. Heat throbbed through his shaft, the pleasure so intense it was almost pain, and he pushed his hips upwards in a roll, his body asking what words were not.

Rory continued to massage his sac, and the fingers of his other hand once again brushed across that special patch of skin behind his balls. Each touch was a shot of searing electricity along every nerve ending in his body. Rory's touch was silk trailing across overheated skin, and when long and delicate fingers wrapped themselves around his hot and engorged cock, Jack released a strangled moan.

The grip was light and loose, but sure. The gentle up-and-down rhythm pushed and pulled his foreskin over the head of his cock, over and over. Jack thrust his hips upwards, into Rory's fisted hand. Jack's tight ab muscles twitched and rippled as heat enveloped him.

"*Ro...*" It was all Jack could grind out. His brain had short-circuited. He couldn't think beyond Rory's mouth, and Rory's hands, and the heat and need between his legs.

Rory's lips formed a tight band around his cock, every soaked slide igniting the delicious nerviness of Jack's shaft. A sweep of Rory's tongue, lapping against the sensitive head, swirling around the crown. A tiny suck, a tiny kiss, Rory's breath hot against his burning, tight flesh, before he was swallowed down to the root.

Jack pressed the heels of his hands against his eyes and saw flashes of white in the darkness. Rory had picked up rhythm and speed, his breathing as hard and ragged as Jack's own as Rory rode him with his mouth. Jack gasped, his hips snapping and jerking as his orgasm built and rose and gathered strength. His balls tingled and tightened, the muscles in his abdomen quivered as his hips thrust up faster. He was rushing towards the point of no return as Rory urged him on and on and on. Jack forced his eyes open, and Rory filled his vision. The surge in Jack's heart made him cry out at the vision of his beautiful fiancé taking him deep into his mouth.

Their eyes met for a second, the connection between them, the need, the heat, the *love,* everything they were together contained in that one moment before Rory dropped his gaze.

God, but I love you so much .. the words in Jack's thoughts travelled to his tongue, but they collapsed into a hard, chest-splitting groan as Rory pulled off from his cock and nuzzled into his groin, taking both balls into his mouth, massaging the heavy, full sac with his lips and tongue.

Moans and whimpers and their shredded, ragged breaths filled the bedroom.

"Ah, Christ." Jack ground out, his voice rough and strained as Rory released him and licked his way up along his cock, the slightest scrape of Rory's teeth sending a delicious and exquisite shudder through every one of Jack's nerves. "Bastard," he grunted out when Rory's muffled laugh rumbled through him, but anything more he might have said broke up and fell away as his pulsing cock was again encased in the hot wetness of Rory's mouth.

Jack's hips snapped up as he fucked his man's mouth hard. Victory burst in his chest as every thrust was answered by Rory's strangled whimpers. The sound sent a heavy vibration coursing through Jack. He was racing towards the edge, and there was nothing that could stop him from tumbling over it.

"Fuck, Ro. Fuck, fuck, f-*uck*..."

Jack's words dissolved into an incomprehensible babble as his hips jerked and his body spasmed, releasing wave after wave of cum into Rory's hungry mouth.

Jack lay panting on the damp sheets. The starbursts that had filled his vision faded, and he forced open his eyes. Rory stared down at him, his face flushed and his lips damp. Jack's heart jolted.

Love deeper than he believed could ever exist entwined and twisted in Jack's heart, and he drifted shaking fingers through Rory's sweat-drenched hair.

Rory smiled and pushed himself up to sit on his knees. His stomach was splattered with his own release, and Jack's heart clenched hard when Rory ran a finger across his abs, gathering up the white stickiness on the tip of a finger. He pressed it to Jack's lips; Jack opened his mouth and sucked, tasting his lover. His cock gave a tiny twitch, but it was all it could do.

"Fresh cream. One of your favourites."

"Yeah," Jack said, letting Rory's finger slip from his mouth. His brain was too punch-drunk to come up with anything else.

"Is that all you can say? That very expensive private education you had really was worth the money, wasn't it?"

"Don't be a smart arse. What do you expect me to say when you've just fried my brain?"

Rory laughed and crossed his arms over Jack's stomach, where he rested his chin. His eyes were bright, and he had a big, beaming smile on his face.

"How come you're always so so..." Jack could barely think; his brains weren't just fried but scrambled, too. "Perky. Afterwards, I mean." Yes, that was the word.

"Perky?" Rory quirked a brow, and his smile broadened.

"Yeah... perky..." Jack's words trailed off. Whatever *he* was, he wasn't perky as his eyes dropped to a close. A touch, as soft and light as a feather, brushed across his lips. Warmth and contentment washed over Jack as he sank into the silky, silent blackness of sleep.

The light snow that had been falling on and off the last couple of days had decided to pack its bags and go. Instead of the heavy cloud-laden sky, all that was above them was the bright blue of a crisp and cold December morning.

When Jack suggested they visit the Christmas Fair at Leadenhall, Rory had nodded with enthusiasm. His eyes had been bright and his smile brighter, and Jack's heart had flipped over. That was the Rory he wanted, not the stressed and worried version.

Even though it was Sunday, the streets were busy and the Tube busier, as people rushed to complete their Christmas shopping. It didn't take long to get to Leadenhall, the beautiful and ornate Victorian arcade deep in the heart of the City of London.

Two huge Christmas trees stood either side of the main entrance. Each was a replica of the other, covered in flickering fairy lights, every bough weighed down with bows and baubles, and on top of each a chubby and cherubic Christmas angel.

"Oh, they're beautiful," Rory said as he stared up at the trees. "We need to put up our own tree. We've been concentrating so much on the shop we've neglected our own home. I love our spindly little plastic tree and all its faded, rubbishy decorations."

Rory started laughing, and Jack gave him a mock glare.

"Are you dissing my tree?"

The cheap plastic tree he'd had since he was a student, along with each trashy decoration and ragged piece of tinsel, held a cherished memory. There was no way they could have Christmas without the tatty old tree taking pride of place in their living room. Rory was right. They needed to get it sorted.

"I would never dare do that. But we could do it later, couldn't we? Afterwards, we can drink far too many snowballs and pig out on warm mince pies."

Rory smiled up into Jack's eyes, and Jack's heart gave a little flip. That's what they had done that first Christmas they were together, just two years before. It seemed both seconds and a lifetime ago.

Jack took Rory's hands into his own and Rory returned the tight squeeze, the only acknowledgement he needed that Rory treasured the memory as much as he did.

"Come on." Rory pulled Jack into the arcade and towards the rows of stalls all selling Christmas-themed food, drink, and gifts. "I want to try some spiced gingerbread and mulled wine."

The arcade was busy, but not yet packed, and they didn't have to push and shove too much to get through the crowds.

"Mmm, this is good," Jack said as he took a sip of the warm, spicy, heady wine as they stood to the side of a stall that looked like it belonged in Hansel and Gretel's world. "I wonder if we could do this in the bakery? Not sell it, but just offer free samples?"

"I'd love to because it'd go really well with our Christmas pudding muffins or our dark chocolate torte, but I'm not sure we'd be allowed. Alcohol, you see. We're not licensed for alcohol. I like the idea, though, of having a license. It'd open up all sorts of possibilities."

Rory sipped and hummed his approval. His brow knitted in a slight frown not of worry but of concentration as he lost himself in thought. Jack bit down on his smile. It was a look he recognised, knowing Rory was thinking the idea over, going through the *what-ifs*.

"If we were a licensed café rather than just a bakery, we could apply for an alcohol license. But we're not." Rory shrugged, and the tiny frown of concentration disappeared.

Jack carried on drinking his mulled wine, barely tasting it. Should he say anything now? Should he outline the thoughts that were turning into plans? Expansion not just into the shop next door to The Bakehouse, which Jack had been told on good authority would soon become vacant, but changing into something else. Not just a bakery but a café too.

With or without an alcohol license. It would work, he was sure of it, not just because he believed in Rory's genius to make it work, but because the numbers added up, too.

The words tingled on the tip of Jack's tongue. They needed to talk, to go into the New Year with bold, bright plans he knew with every bone in his body would succeed. Jack licked his lips and turned to Rory, who was looking around him with a big carefree smile on his face, revelling in the festive scene all around them. The words, for now, at least, would remain a tingle.

They went from stall to stall, nibbling, sipping, tasting all the little samples on hand. They bought a few things, including an orange and almond cake and a cupcake topped with a dark chocolate and liquorice frosting.

"Now, this is even weirder than our gin and tonic cupcake." Jack piled some of the frosting onto his fingertip, inspecting it briefly before popping it into his mouth.

"Good, though," Rory said, doing the same. "It's really nice and very unusual. I'm sure I could replicate it but give it our own twist, and with a bit more of a liquorice kick. It's dark and intense; it would be a good addition to our seasonal range. What do you reckon? Should we add this to our Christmas cupcakes?"

Rory stared at him with an intensity Jack knew came from an idea that had moved on to a certainty, before Rory began pulling off pieces of the cupcake, examining it like a scientist would a specimen in the lab.

Jack laughed. "If you eat any more, there won't be any left for you to experiment with back at The Bakehouse."

Rory shook his head. "I won't need to have it with me, because I'll remember the taste." Rory stuffed what was left of the cupcake into his mouth and hummed in appreciation.

Jack smiled because how could he not when Rory was so enthusiastic and fired up? This was how he wanted him to be, *needed* him to be. *After Christmas, after the wedding...*

"You know, with all these free samples, I don't think I want any lunch. Do you mind?"

Jack shook his head. "No, I'm fine, but I could do with a coffee, though." He nodded to a coffee cart near where they had bought the cupcakes. "Grab those seats over there, and I'll go get us a drink."

As Jack made his way across and stood in the queue, his thoughts drifted to what he had planned for next. Coming to Leadenhall hadn't just been about the Christmas Fair.

Earlier in the week, he'd made a special delivery to

the offices of an art agency, and all the hipster girls and boys had *oohed* and *aahed* over the mini Christmas cakes and Yule logs they'd ordered for a client event that evening. But Jack hadn't headed straight back to The Bakehouse. Instead, he'd made a detour to a tiny, narrow, winding side street, to a shop with a plain sign over the door which read *Hogarth & Son*.

A tiny shop in a tinier street, specialising in rare and antique watches. Jack's jaw had dropped when he'd called in and the elder Mr. Hogarth had shown him the watch. It was a near-replica of the one he himself wore, with only a few minor differences. It was perfect, or nearly; all it needed was the engraving. Jack had received the call the day before. Yes, Mr. De Lacy, he had been told, the shop would be open for collection on Sunday, between the hours of ten and three…

After their coffee, they made their way around the rest of the market. Rory stopped, transfixed by a stall selling handmade decorations.

"What do you think?" Rory held up a punk rocker fairy, complete with spiky rainbow hairdo, and a safety pin through her nose.

Jack cocked his head to the side. "Well, now that Doris spends all her time at the bakery, we need somebody to take her place at the top of the tree at home. I reckon a punk rocker fairy could do it."

"I knew you'd see sense," Rory said, laughing.

They paid for the punk rocker fairy and picked up a few more decorations just as individual and idiosyncratic and all perfect for their little tree.

There wasn't much more to see in the Leadenhall, and it was getting uncomfortably crowded, so Jack eased them out from the press of bodies. On the street, they pulled on their gloves and wound their scarves tighter. The bright clear day was as cold as ever, and every breath they took billowed in the still and frosty air. Taking Rory's hand, Jack led him away.

"Where are we going? The Tube station's that way." Rory nodded in the direction they were coming from.

"We're not going home, or not just yet."

"Oh? I thought we were going to decorate our living room, drink lots of advocaat, and then get naked on the rug."

Jack threw back his head and laughed. "That sounds like a plan, but there's something I want to do first."

"You mean something is more important than naked advocaat?"

Jack just smiled in response. There wasn't a lot that was more important than naked advocaat, but what they were about to do next just about topped it.

The tiny street would be so easy to miss in the

messy and higgledy-piggledy maze that was the City of London.

"Jack? What—?"

Jack pressed his fingertips to Rory's lips and gazed into Rory's questioning, confused eyes.

"Just go with me on this, okay?"

Jack pushed the door open, and he and Rory stepped into another time.

The shop was crammed with tall and narrow display cabinets, all of them holding a treasure of watches. Behind the counter, in a corner and almost hidden, sat a small, round, bald-headed man. A pair of glasses perched on the end of his nose, and another was wedged on the top of his head as he worked on the mechanism of a pocket watch, using what looked like a set of toy tools.

"Mr. De Lacy." The man put aside his work, stood up and extended his hand to Jack.

"Mr. Hogarth. Let me introduce Rory Kincaid, my fiancé."

Jack moved aside to allow Rory to shake Mr. Hogarth's hand. Jack smiled; in a moment everything would be revealed.

"Let me bring your order." Mr. Hogarth disappeared into a back room.

"Jack, I don't understand. What's going on?"

Before Jack could answer, Mr. Hogarth returned

bearing a small black box, which he handed over to Jack.

"Please." Mr. Hogarth gestured to a small table and a couple of chairs on the other side of the shop, in the only space not taken up with display cabinets, before he returned to his place once more behind the counter and took up his work as though he were alone.

"I want you to have this," Jack said, opening the box as soon as he and Rory were seated.

"What?" Rory gaped at the watch, displayed on a pad of black velvet. "But we agreed a strict ten-pound budget, just something silly this year. I haven't—"

"No, it's not a Christmas present."

"Then what—? I don't understand."

Jack took the watch out of the box. Like his own, it was plain and unadorned. The black Roman numerals were stark against the white face; the casing was gold, deep and burnished.

"When I was twenty-one, my father presented me with a watch from this shop. He did the same for George," Jack said, referring to his elder brother. "My father also had a watch on his twenty-first birthday, as did my grandfather, great-grandfather, and great-greatgrandfather. The De Lacy men have had watches in one form or another from Hogarth's since the late eighteenth century. All those watches came from here, from this very shop." Jack glanced toward the counter, but Mr. Hogarth had gone and was now nowhere to be seen.

"This isn't a Christmas present, Ro. This is something every De Lacy man receives. And I wanted you to have one, too, because that's what you're on the point of becoming: a De Lacy man." Jack's lips lifted in a wry smile. "I didn't know you when you turned twenty-one, although I wish I did I'm just making up for lost time. On Christmas Eve, you're going to take my name. I want you to be wearing this watch when you do."

"Jack, I–I don't know what to say."

"Then don't say anything. Just accept it, along with the words I had engraved."

Jack held the watch out. All his focus was on his fiancé, reading for the first time the words engraved not only on the watch but on Jack's heart.

Love, always and forever.

Four simple words which said everything Jack held deep inside about the man he'd found huddled on his doorstep just two Christmases before.

"Here, let me put it on you." Jack cleared his throat. His voice was rougher and more gravelly than he'd meant it to be as he took the watch and turned Rory's wrist.

Rory nodded, keeping his head bowed, but Jack

saw his Adam's apple bobbing up and down, and smiled.

"It's beautiful," Rory said. "Perfect. I don't know what to say."

"Just accept it."

"You give me so much, Jack." Rory looked up, and Jack's heart burst deep in his chest.

Rory's eyes glittered, and a lone tear fell, making its slow and meandering journey down his cheek. He leant forward and brushed a gentle kiss to Jack's lips. It was the softest, sweetest, and most heartfelt kiss Rory had ever given him. Jack took his fiancé's face between his hands and brushed away the solitary tear with his thumb before he pressed his brow to Rory's.

"I love you, Rory Kincaid. So. Bloody. Much." Jack separated each word with a kiss.

"I trust everything is to your satisfaction?"

Jack dragged his attention from Rory to the watchmaker, who stood on the other side of the counter across the small shop, a benign smile on his face, his hands clasped loosely across his middle.

"Yes. Thank you. It's perfect."

"It is," Rory added.

Mr. Hogarth nodded and smiled. With goodbyes and season's greetings, Jack and Rory left the quiet and shadowy shop and stepped out into the narrow street, bright under the cold winter sunlight.

Jack took Rory's hand in his. There was no need to say anything, but even if he'd wanted to, he doubted he would've been able. His throat had closed up, too full of emotion. A quick glance at Rory revealed his fiancé's still glittering eyes. They had no need for words as they headed to the Tube and towards home.

CHAPTER EIGHT

Rory gazed down at the watch, loosely wrapped around his wrist like a warm hand.

He'd been completely overcome in the watchmaker's little shop. All he'd had before was a cheap digital watch, bought some years ago for not even a tenner from a street market selling tat. But this was perfect; nothing showy, nothing flash, just a plain white-faced watch with black numerals, and pure class. Too classy for him, maybe, but Rory shoved the thought aside.

A small bubble of intimidation had burst in his stomach when Jack had said the De Lacy men were always given a watch from Hogarth's. Okay, that might have been on each and every De Lacy man's twenty-first birthday, but it was as much a right of passage as his forthcoming wedding would be.

A De Lacy man. It was a heady thought. A year ago to the day almost, since Jack had asked him to be his husband. He'd had a full year to get used to the idea, but it still made his heart beat faster and his mouth dry up. In overwhelming happiness, at least most of the time. But not always, and it filled him with guilt. He continued to stare down at the watch, held on his wrist by a soft and supple leather strap, his thoughts twisting and turning.

The De Lacys, an ancient family backed up by history and tradition. Sometimes Rory asked himself what he, a man with no history other than that given to him by his adoptive parents, whom he had long ago lost contact with, could bring to such a family. He'd come and stood before them with nothing other than Jack's love, and they had accepted him.

Accepted him.

It sounded begrudging and that wasn't what it was, not at all. Jack's parents, after a small misstep, had declared him one of their own. But sometimes, just sometimes, and in his quietest moments, he couldn't help but wonder if they questioned their youngest child's choice, if they asked themselves why Jack hadn't bestowed his love on someone more appropriate, someone more like *them*.

Why was he even thinking such things? Shame

stabbed at him. The De Lacy family had not just accepted him, it had wrapped its arms around him and held him tight.

Nerves. That's all it was. Wedding nerves, a battling mix of fear and excitement as the most important day of his life loomed. But the thoughts he'd shoved aside tugged at his sleeve and tapped on his shoulder.

Rory jumped and swung around as the front door slammed.

"Got the lemonade," Jack said with a grin as he strode into the living room. "You can't make a snowball without lemonade. You okay?"

"Sure. Just hankering after my snowball. Anyway," Rory said, mentally booting his troubling thoughts in the backside, "you can't get naked on the rug with all this on." He unbuttoned Jack's heavy winter coat and tugged it from his shoulders.

Jack laughed. "Easy, tiger. We've got a tree to decorate and snowballs to make before we get up close and personal with the rug. Ah, see you got it up all right. In a manner of speaking." Jack's eyes fell to the spindly plastic Christmas tree standing by the side of the fireplace, his smile growing wider.

Rory followed his gaze. "Just about. It's a bit wonky, though."

"It was always wonky, now it's just a bit wonkier. This tree has so much history."

Jack trailed his fingers along the plastic pine needles. He had a distant and dreamy expression spread across his face. A small sadness panged in Rory's heart. Jack was remembering all the happy times associated with the little tree, and Rory only wished he could have shared in those times with him. How different and how much better both their lives would have been.

"Here," Rory said, picking up a battered cardboard box. "We've got more decorations here than we have tree. Maybe we should just pick out one or two things and go for the minimalist approach." Rory deliberately ignored the look of abject horror he knew Jack was throwing his way as he sorted through the beaten and battered decorations.

"You're sailing close to the wind, Kincaid. I don't know if I can trust you with the tree. You might try and put something classy on it." Jack shuddered, over the top and theatrical, but his face broke out into a grin.

They emptied the box of decorations onto the rug and knelt down, sorting through the stars, Santas, Christmas angels, and glitter-covered bells. And gnomes wearing Santa hats. The gnomes had been bought the previous year; kitschy and tacky, they had made the perfect addition. Rory picked one up and considered it.

"Do you think the punk rocker fairy is fit for such august company?"

The alternative Christmas fairy had seemed a good idea, back at Leadenhall market, but compared to the rest of the tat scattered around them, it was far too smart. The tree and its decorations were all about over the top, overdone, in-your-face tackiness. If the decorated Christmas tree was a drag queen, it would be a drag queen after too much gin, staggering home in the early hours with her wig knocked sideways and her makeup running.

"I think she'll make a wonderful replacement for Doris." Jack plucked the fairy from Rory's hand. "I love that she's snarling and has a safety pin through her nose, and she looks like she'd stuff that wand right up where the sun doesn't shine."

Rory laughed. Yes, Jack had a point. The punk rocker fairy had attitude. If she was going to grant three wishes, they would have to be big, bad, and very, very dirty.

"What shall we call her? She has to have a name."

Jack tilted his head and narrowed his eyes. "Bunty."

Rory coughed and snorted at once. "Excuse me? Bunty? Er, why?"

"Because she is so *not* a Bunty." Jack sat back on his haunches, and studied the plaster fairy.

Rory smiled as he shook his head. "Are you sure you haven't been having a few nips of advocaat?"

"Now there's a good idea. You sort out the decorations—and don't forget the rainbow feather boa—while I go and make a jug of snowball." Jack's nose twitched, and he breathed in deep. "Ah, good, you've got the mince pies heating." Jack dashed off to the kitchen.

Rory sorted through the scattered decorations. Not that it would've made any difference, because every single one of them would end up on the tree, with the rainbow feather boa wound around last of all. If the gaudily decorated tree had been Jack's tradition before he had come on the scene, then a jug of snowball and a plate of warm mince pies was *their* tradition, one they had created at their first Christmas together.

The feather boa slipped from Rory's hands. He stared down at the baubles and decorations, the glitter faded and disintegrating.

"These will be too hot to eat," Jack said, bursting into the living room. "We'll have to leave them for a minute or so." Jack dumped the tray piled high with mince pies, the jug of snowball, and two glasses, on the coffee table. "Ro? What's the matter?"

"Nothing... Nothing at all."

Jack dropped to his knees next to him. "You don't fool me, Kincaid. What's up?"

"I know I don't. I'm not sure why I even bother trying. I was just thinking about how much things have changed, since we met."

"The business, you mean, and getting married?"

"No. Smaller things, I suppose."

Rory shivered as Jack's fingers rubbed and circled through his hair, and he pushed himself into the strong, sure touch.

"Like making new traditions," Rory said after a moment or two of silence. "Decorating the tree as we drink snowballs and eat mince pies, for instance. That's a tradition we've made together."

"Making things that are uniquely and only ours."

"Yes." Rory shifted and looked up into Jack's steady blue-eyed gaze. He laid his hand against Jack's stubble-roughened cheek. "They make me feel safe and whole and complete," he said quietly. "I never felt those things, not really, until I met you. I know it sounds silly—"

"No, it's not silly. I suppose it was like you were waiting for somebody to make those traditions with you. When I was with Sam, we didn't make traditions, we fought against them. I can see that now. Like the tree." Jack nodded towards it. "He hated it and wanted to replace it with a bunch of twigs in a poncy vase with just a couple of puny white lights hanging from them. He always wanted things one way, and I wanted them another. You can't make traditions when you're fighting each other. You've got to be acting in harmony."

Sam, Jack's betraying, deceitful ex-boyfriend. The man had faded into history and become nothing.

"Come on," Jack said, standing up and extending a hand to Rory. "Let's celebrate our tradition."

It didn't take long to decorate the small tree. Every plastic branch was weighed down with every single decoration before the rainbow feather boa was wound around and around. But there was one more touch needed, the crowning glory: Bunty, the punk rocker fairy. They stepped back to inspect their handiwork.

Jack grinned. "As gaudy, tacky, and bad taste as ever. And long may that be the case. We need to toast the tree."

Jack poured them each a glass of snowball, and they clinked glasses before raising them to the tree and taking a sip of the egg yolk yellow cocktail.

Although it was only three-thirty in the afternoon, the clear blue sky was already fading into a deep purple bruise. The only light was that cast by the crackling fire and the string of deep blue fairy lights draped along the mantelpiece. The room was warm, the snowball rich and spiced, and the mince pies buttery and crumbly, their vine fruit filling sweet and sharp at the same time. But best of all, Jack had slipped his arm around his shoulder and pulled him in tight to his body. Rory snuggled closer. The moment was perfect, and Rory never wanted it to end.

"What happened to getting naked on the rug?" Jack asked.

"I'll trade you two lots of nakedness later for a snuggle now. How does that sound?"

"It'll have to do, I suppose," Jack said with an exaggerated sigh.

Rory put his glass down before he plucked Jack's from his hand, and pushed him down into the sofa's plump cushions. He smiled as he climbed into Jack's lap.

"Maybe I'm being too hasty."

Rory's hands trailed over Jack, making their way south. He pressed down on the growing bulge between Jack's legs.

"Yes, you shouldn't be too hasty." Jack flexed his hips upwards, pushing into Rory's hand.

Naked. On the rug, on the sofa, in the bed. Suddenly it sounded like a very good idea, and Rory didn't care where, just as long as it happened and happened quick.

Rory's fingers flew to the front of Jack's shirt, scrambling to unbutton and reach the warm flesh, stretched taut over hard muscle. He shifted around so he was straddling his fiancé's lap. His hips undulated in a soft roll, each back-and-forward movement rubbing over Jack's hard and heavy cock. Jack sucked in a shaky breath and Rory smiled before he crushed his lips to Jack's.

The sweet, spice-laced kiss was deep and dark, wet and sloppy, and as rich and heady as Christmas itself.

Jack mumbled something incoherent, but Rory didn't need to understand the words to know their meaning. He pinched Jack's nipples, twisting hard, smiling against Jack's lips as a shudder shimmered through his man. It was his turn to shudder when Jack's hands grasped his arse, his fingers rubbing and kneading at his denim covered flesh.

Jack bucked his hips, and Rory slipped from his lap and shuffled between Jack's splayed legs. Rory glanced up, his eyes met Jack's and he swallowed at the dark need he saw reflected in their depths.

"Got to finish what you started, Ro."

Jack's voice was rough and low as he thrust his hips forward. It was all Rory needed to yank him out of the split second of stillness he'd fallen into, and his hands flew to Jack's belt.

Unbuckled, Rory attacked the buttons before he eased the zip over the bulge pushing at the front of Jack's jeans. Rory licked his lips at the outline of Jack's swollen cock trapped beneath his briefs. He pressed his face against Jack's heat, breathing in the deep, heavy, musky scent of the man he loved so much, before he drew back and palmed Jack's shaft.

"Ro," Jack croaked, his voice shaking and gravelly with want. "I—"

The door bell's ring was a diamond-sharp knife cutting through the heavy, dense air.

Rory's hand froze, wrapped around Jack's cotton-clad dick. He looked up, and Jack stared down at him with wide eyes.

"What the—? Oh, *shit*," Jack grumbled.

And then Rory remembered too. Four o'clock, and the start of carols around the tree set up on the little patch of green in the square below.

"Can't we pretend we're not here?" Jack looked at him through beseeching eyes.

Rory shook his head, but Jack already knew the answer — as did his dick, softening in Rory's hand.

"You're the outgoing chairman. You have to be there, to hand over the baton." Rory shifted, releasing Jack's now deflated cock.

"The only baton I'm interested in at the moment is the one you've got your hand around. Or did have."

"I know. I'd better get the door, while you, er…"

The bell rang again, and this time whoever was on

the other side of the door was keeping their finger pressed on the button.

Rory dashed from the living room, closing the door behind him. Plastering a smile to his face, he slung open the front door and was met with the toothy grin of their downstairs neighbour, treasurer of the Residents' Association and enthusiastic organiser of the carol concert.

"I was beginning to think you were out. But then I thought, no, Jack and Rory wouldn't forget." Trevor's smile grew bigger. "It's starting in ten minutes, and we can't start without the chairman." Trevor's smile almost split his face in two, and he didn't bother hiding that he was peering over Rory's shoulder into the flat.

Thank God I closed the door... "Sorry. We were, er, sorting out our decorations. We kind of lost track of time." It was true, every word of it. "Give us a few minutes, and we'll be down."

Trevor nodded, and stood on tiptoes to peer over Rory's shoulder once more.

"Guess who that was," Rory said to a grumpy-looking Jack.

"Toothy Trev." Jack huffed. "Couldn't you have told him I had more pressing things on my mind and in my pants?" Jack looked down at this groin, and Rory laughed.

"We'll just have to save the getting naked on the

rug until later. A rousing chorus of Oh Come All Ye Faithful can do wonders for the libido, or so I've been told."

"Depends what kind of come you're talking about." Jack got up and adjusted himself under his jeans.

Minutes later, they were heading downstairs and out into the square.

CHAPTER NINE

Rory clutched two large Tupperware boxes, one packed with little squares of chocolate, caramel, and sour cherry brownies, and the other with mince pies.

It had been freezing cold all day, but the early evening air snatched Rory's breath away. The temperature had plummeted. He glanced up at the sky. The very last light had faded into inky blackness, leaving a scattering of stars glittering against the dark.

The little tucked-away square was filling up with their fellow residents, but also those from the warren of small streets that radiated outwards.

"We're so lucky to live here."

"I suppose so," Jack muttered.

"There's no suppose about it. There's a sense of

community, and that's rarer than you think. I grew up in a small town, but nobody knew the neighbours, and no way would anything like this happen. Look," Rory said, pointing. "There's Trevor. He's waving at us. Do your duty as the outgoing chairman, greet the neighbours and wish them a happy Christmas. And if you behave, I might be able to arrange a bit of rug time later," he added under his breath.

Jack gave an extravagant sigh. "Rug time, but only if I speak to Trevor? You're a cruel man, Kincaid. Just please don't leave me alone with him."

Rory sniggered. "But he loves you. I swear his grin gets bigger and his teeth get more buck every time he sees you."

"I hoped you hadn't noticed that," Jack said on a groan. "Those teeth of his give me nightmares. Imagine the damage they could cause if they got to within an inch of my—"

"Jack," Trevor said as he strode across, clutched Jack's arm and pulled him forward. "Now you're here, we need to get everybody a drink and then gather for the carols."

Rory smiled and waggled his fingers as Jack threw him a silent *help me* as Trevor dragged him away.

Rory looked around. There were a good fifty people in the square, if not more. Pride of place was taken by a huge Scotch pine, set up on the small patch of green, and its white fairy lights twinkled on and off in the cold night air. At the pinnacle was a large silver star, and at its base, models of Santa, his elf helpers and reindeers and a sleigh. Small children pointed and laughed, and tried to grab at the Lapland scene, held back by smiling parents.

We are lucky to live here. So, so lucky...

Rory sought out Jack in the crowd, and found him immediately when he heard sudden raucous laughter: Jack, in the middle of the knot of men and women who led the Residents' Association, a wide smile on his face as a glass of steaming mulled wine was pushed on him. Rory smiled. In the middle of a huge and anonymous city, that neighbours had gathered to celebrate the season together, it was something to be held close and celebrated.

"Oh, are they goodies from The Bakehouse?"

A woman with a Peruvian-style hat with long tassels hanging from ear flaps eyed the boxes Rory was still clutching.

Rory scrambled to remember her name. She'd moved in over the summer and had thrown herself into the life of the square with gusto.

"Jodie." She gave Rory a wide grin, clearly unbothered he'd forgotten her name.

"Yes, they are. I'd better put them out." Rory nodded towards a collapsible table that stood a few yards off.

"Thank goodness there's going to be something edible, let alone delicious. Monica has supplied vegan snacks." Jodie pronounced *vegan snacks* as though the words were in quotation marks.

Rory caught her eye, and they both laughed as they shuddered at the same time. They, and the other residents of the square, had been subjected to the dry-as-dust and heavy-as-brick healthy meat alternatives at a recent fundraiser.

The brownies and mince pies joined the rest of the contributions laid out on the table. Along with Monica's vegan snacks, which bore a little flag on top proclaiming themselves to be proudly animal-free, there were homemade sausage rolls, a heap of jacket potatoes, and what looked suspiciously like some kind of quinoa salad along with various bean-based dips.

Jodie nodded at the unseasonable salad and dips. "They'll end up going in the bin." She didn't bother to lower her voice. "Who wants salads in the middle of winter? It's Christmas, and everybody wants to take onboard as much fat and sugar as they can," she said, laughing.

"At least people have made the effort..." Rory said in defence, but he reckoned she was right.

There was also stollen, what he thought was a Yule log, and a Christmas cake that looked like somebody had tried to represent the square, judging by the decorations on top. Rory grinned. It was almost impossible to look at food without casting a professional eye. Much of the food looked a mess, no two ways, but it didn't matter; what *did* was that the community had come together. Yes, he and Jack weren't just lucky, they were privileged to be a part of that.

Rory turned to speak to Jodie, and found her lavishing all her attention on a golden labrador puppy. Rory's heart melted. The puppy reminded him so much of a young Badger, would-be Nativity scene sheep, and biter of the vicar's arse.

"Here you go, have this."

Jack appeared in front of him, and thrust a steaming glass of mulled wine into his hand.

"Ro? You okay? You've got a seriously dopey expression on your face."

Rory rolled his eyes. "Dopey? I was just looking at that young puppy, that's all. He reminds me so much of Badger."

Jack snorted. "The little bugger dug a hole and buried my trainers the last time we were at my parents'," Jack said as he sipped his drink.

"I do miss him, though."

"I know," Jack said, his voice soft and low. "If we

lived in a house and had a garden, I'd have no hesitation about bringing him back here to live with us. But until then—"

"Jack, Rory," a man called, striding across, a half-eaten mince pie in his hand. "Top notch baking as usual..."

Others joined them. The talk was a mixture of what everybody was going to be doing for the Christmas holiday, and his and Jack's wedding. The buzz of voices around them was filled with laughter, fuelled by the heady and highly alcoholic mulled wine. The table holding the refreshments was mobbed, and Rory lost count of the number of compliments he received for the contribution from The Bakehouse. Even the quinoa salad had more takers than Monica's vegan snacks.

"Ladies and gentlemen, girls and boys, if I could have your attention, please."

Rory and Jack, along with everybody else, turned their attention to an elderly gentleman standing in front of the Christmas tree. His voice wasn't loud, but it was clear and commanding; it was a voice that expected to be listened to. Rory knew him to be in his eighties, but with his intelligent, bright eyes, the years had no claim on him. The man's heavy white beard, big round the body, and bright red coat and peaked red hat, made him a living, breathing Santa Claus.

"I'm Stanley, as I think you all know. As the oldest resident of the square and one of the original founders of the Association, it falls upon me to thank everybody for attending this evening to enjoy some neighbourly festive cheer. We have gathered around the tree to sing carols every year since 1962, years before many of you were even born. It's a tradition I'm proud to see continue, and just as strong as ever."

The gathered crowd, as one, paused in its eating and drinking to burst into applause.

Rory glanced up at Jack, and warmth spread through his heart. His fiancé had half a sausage roll sticking out his mouth and was attempting to clap at the same time he was holding his mulled wine, sloshing some from the glass. Even in the low light cast from the Christmas tree's twinkly lights and the few street lights dotted around the square, Rory could see that Jack was flushed from more than the sharp night air. Carols around the tree, the Easter egg hunt in the local park, and the summer fête may not have been traditions as old and ingrained as those which took place in Jack's home village of Polton Lacy, but they were just as important to the group gathered here tonight.

Stanley was saying something else, and Rory raced to catch up. A quick squeeze on his shoulder, and Jack was pushing through the crowd.

The applause grew louder and Stanley was

pumping Jack's hand in an enthusiastic handshake. Trevor the toothy neighbour had joined them, and they stood in a line and smiled into a huge, professional-looking camera. Two others joined them, one of whom was Jodie, and more handshaking ensued as the chairman and treasurer stepped down to make way for their successors.

"And now, we have what you have all been eagerly waiting for: this year's carol concert around the tree." Stanley's announcement was greeted with more clapping and cheers. "Monica is distributing song sheets, but these are all old favourites, and I'm sure you already know the words. Our good friends Heidi, Cathy, and Lesley, as star members of the South London Operatic Society, will start by giving us a couple of rousing choruses of Jingle Bells to get us all going. Although with all the mulled wine that has already been drunk," he added to a background of laughter, "I think you're already quite in the mood."

The trio, to loud and enthusiastic applause, readied themselves, hands folded loosely across their middles, when Monica bustled up to Stanley and whispered in his ear.

"Oh, erm, before we begin, Monica has asked me to remind you all that there are still plenty of vegan snacks to be eaten, and that she remains open for orders for Christmas and New Year's parties."

Monica, an ageing hippie in a flowing caftan, her long frizzy hair threaded with silver, smiled out at the gathering. Earlier, Rory had discreetly disposed of something oily and bitter, with a spurious claim to be an onion bhaji, which she'd thrust into his hand. He grimaced, and doubted she'd be getting too many orders that evening. He forgot it all when arms entwined around his waist, arms he'd have known anywhere. He pushed back into Jack's firm body.

Heidi, Cathy, and Lesley's clear soprano voices climbed up into the heavens. Accompanied only by a violinist, the performance was breathtaking. A couple of choruses and the women were done, smiling graciously as everybody erupted into enthusiastic and deafening cheering and clapping.

"Best do my duty as the outgoing chairman," Jack whispered in his ear and, a second later, was gone as he joined the other Residents' Association members as they made their way through the crowd topping up drinks, which helped lubricate the voices as everybody sang along to the popular and well-loved carols.

Rory sang, too, his voice joining the others ringing around the square. He could carry a tune, but his voice was nothing like Jack's. As he made his way through the crowd, Jack's voice rang out, unmistakeable in its clarity, depth and strength. 'The product of years of singing in the church choir,' he always said. 'Nothing at all to do with all those music lessons at your very expensive and very exclusive private school, then?' Rory had teased, the first time he had really heard Jack's voice. Wherever it was Jack had learned to sing, it didn't matter. His voice was as beautiful as the man himself.

Rory's voice faltered, and his eyes misted over, and he blinked hard to clear his vision.

The happy scene in the square was Christmas card perfect. The big traditional tree, decked only in simple lights, the solid Victorian houses lit up with candles and fairy lights, all cast a warm glow into the square. Along with the Christmas carols, the warm winter spice from the mulled wine added to the feeling of community and tradition. And *he* was part of it, when not so long before he'd been part of nothing and wanted by nobody.

He searched around, desperate suddenly for a sight of his man. Jack was laughing with somebody, but as though to a silent call, he turned his head and looked directly at Rory, their eyes locking as Jack smiled... *I'm here and always will be...* Everything and everyone faded away, and for a moment it was only the two of them. The little swell of panic in Rory's chest subsided, and the sounds of the square rushed back in.

The Christmas carols came to an end. The mulled wine had been drunk to the last drop, and the refreshments eaten; even the huge pile of vegan snacks had gone down. A little. Everybody who had bought something to share retrieved their bowls, tins, and plates. A surge of satisfaction filled Rory when he didn't even find a crumb left in his Tupperware boxes.

"Julie and Eddie are having a party." Jack appeared at his side and nodded to their neighbours, who lived in the biggest and grandest house on the square. "Did you want to...?"

"I think I'd rather go home, to be honest. Just me, you, and Bunty."

Jack laughed, throwing his head back. "I was hoping you'd say that. But a threesome, eh? Not sure what I think of that because I don't like the idea of sharing you."

"Not even with a punk rocker fairy?"

"Not even with the air you breathe, or the sun, or the sky, or the moon—"

"You've had too many mulled wines," Rory said, laughing. "I've a feeling you might be a little bit drunk. I like it."

"The only thing I'm drunk on, Rory Kincaid, is you."

Rory's eyes drifted closed as Jack pressed his lips to his. The sweet spice of the heated wine mixed with the taste of Jack himself. It was a slow and gentle kiss, full of more love than Rory thought he would ever have. It was perfect, because it was Jack.

"Let's go home." Jack held out his hand to Rory.

Home. That one little word would never grow old, because home was where Jack was. Rory clasped his hand to Jack's and let him lead them both away.

CHAPTER TEN

"Oh shit." Why had he insisted on having two large snowballs when they got back to the flat the night before? Jack couldn't really remember much after that, but a hazy memory of having a brandy nightcap or three after the snowballs surfaced through the fog of his brain.

He stretched and scratched along the base of his stomach. His fingernails came away with something flaky under the nails. He stared at them. Had it been him, Rory, and Bunty after all? He must've been plastered if he couldn't remember a night with Rory.

Rory. Where was he?

The place next to him in the bed was cold, which didn't bode well. *How long have I slept for?* He pushed himself up onto his elbows and squinted at the bedside cabinet clock.

Christ. It was after 9 o'clock, which meant the bakery had already been open for over an hour. Jack flopped back into the bed and groaned. Rory wasn't going to be happy with him, and he couldn't blame him. The shop would already be heaving with customers, and it needed all hands on board with everybody fighting fit.

"And I'm neither," he mumbled into the silent air.

Jack staggered up from bed, and every step he took pounded in his head. When had he last had such a bad hangover? He didn't know what he needed first of all the most: a shower, a coffee, or a handful of painkillers. All three, probably, and in a massive dose. He scratched at the itch tingling across his stomach, at the flaking, dried cum under his nails. It made the decision for him.

The hot shower went some way to making him feel human again, but Jack still needed coffee and painkillers to complete the holy trinity. In the kitchen, his phone sat on the table alongside the empty jug of snowball and the used glasses. He grabbed it and found the text message he'd hoped would be there.

Thought it was safer to leave you snoring, Sleeping Beauty XXX

So-*oo*, Rory couldn't be too pissed off with him, could he? No, not if he was leaving him kisses. Jack jabbed speed dial and seconds later, was connected to Rory.

"You should've woken me up." Jack's opening words were met with a low laugh.

"I tried, but you were dead to the world. The safest course of action was to leave you to sleep it off."

"I'm really sorry, I shouldn't have got pissed. I know how busy we are and—"

"No, you shouldn't have, and yes we are — and we do need you here as soon as."

"Okay. Sorry."

Rory chuckled. "You're forgiven. This time. Mabel's been a godsend, as usual. Everything was ready and prepped for this morning, and she and Lance have been working the counter, leaving me to get on with baking."

So everybody had been hard at work while he snored away his hangover... Jack was feeling shittier than he had when he first woke up.

"I'll be with you in half an hour."

Only five or six people were waiting to be served when Jack walked into the bakery. Mabel greeted him with a tiny arch of her brows and a knowing quirk of her scarlet-painted lips. At the same time, she flirted outrageously with the guy who worked in the art supplies shop a couple of streets away; he returned her attentions with a fixed smile and a look of fear in his eyes, and Jack didn't blame him.

Lance served another of their regular customers, his attention fixed on the chatty young woman, doing everything not to return the glances the art supplies guy — *Russ? Guss?* — tried to throw his way. Jack chuckled under his breath. The Bakehouse's teenage apprentice really did need a few lessons, but not in producing the lightest Victoria sponge sandwich or the perfect crusty sourdough loaf.

Jack walked into the warm steam of the kitchen and was enveloped by the delicious aroma of trays of muffins, Danish pastries and croissants sitting on the cooling rack.

"Morning, Sleeping Beauty. Or should I say the Kraken awakes?"

Rory poured ingredients into the industrial food mixer, his hands flour-dusted and his apron splattered with frosting. He had every right to be pissed off, but instead his lips lifted in mild amusement.

"You're going to make me pay for oversleeping, aren't you?"

"Oh yes," Rory said, his voice bright and cheery as

he switched on the mixer. The sound ground into Jack's head like a pneumatic drill. "I'm going to milk it for everything it's worth. Are you up to piping? I need steady hands, though."

Jack scrabbled around in his brain for a suitable response. There was a risqué joke there, some innuendo, but his brain was too sluggish to find it. He held out his hands. They were steady because all the shaking was happening in his head.

Rory laughed as he set out the ingredients and the piping bag.

"The dark chocolate cupcakes need to be topped with Christmas pudding buttercream. Do you remember the proportions?" Rory studied him, and Jack had to resist the urge to squirm and say *Yes, Sir*. Rory had his serious teacher's face on.

"Yes, of course I do. You know I make the best Christmas pudding buttercream out of all of us." Jack said it with a confidence he didn't feel.

"Good. I've got another treacle tart to make, and then I've got three Christmas cakes to decorate. Take your time with the icing. I don't mind them going out a little bit late if need be, but they have to look perfect."

"Yes, Sir. Whatever you say, Sir," Jack mumbled to himself.

Rory was in strict professional baker mode. His fiancé was an endearing mix of courage and reticence, but when he was in his kitchen, Rory was the master of his realm as he strove for perfection in every bake, cake, cookie, or crumble-topped pie that made its way from the oven to the front counter.

Jack weighed and measured the ingredients into another industrial-sized mixer. To the creamed butter and sugar mixture, he added the mixed spice, breathing in deep the warm scent of nutmeg, cinnamon, and allspice. With the tiny drop of brandy, just enough to give the frosting an extra kick, it was the essence of Christmas. Along with the gin and tonic cupcakes, and a couple of other lines, the Christmas pudding cupcakes were marked as strictly for adults. Before he loaded the buttercream into the piping bag, Jack took a teaspoon to taste it. Tasting food as you went along was one of the most important things you could do in the kitchen, Rory always said. Jack had tasted this particular combo dozens of times before, as he'd licked it off Rory's stomach, kissed it from Rory's lips, and sucked it from his—

The clatter of the oven door opening and another batch of cupcakes deposited on the cooling rack yanked Jack out of his buttercream-induced daydream.

"Jack."

Rory nodded to the already cooled cupcakes awaiting icing, and tilted his head. Yes, there was no doubt Rory was in professional baking mode, and Jack knew better than to waste time daydreaming. Not that imagining Rory slathered over with various flavours of buttercream could ever be called a waste of time...

Jack fixed the right sized nozzle, filled the piping bag, and set to work.

He enjoyed mixing up the buttercream and was now trusted to pipe up most of the cupcakes they sold in the bakery. Cake decoration, even in its simplest format, Rory always said, was an art form in its own right.

How hard could it be to top off a little sponge cake with a dollop of frosting? Jack had soon found out the answer when he had made mess after mess of that simple little swirl on endless sheets of baking parchment before he was allowed to go anywhere near a cupcake.

Rory had taught him at home, after hours, and not during the bakery's busy day.

He'd been a hard taskmaster as he'd made Jack repeat and repeat and repeat, never giving him any slack as he had made him practice until Jack had begun to dream of being chased across a field by a giant blob of buttercream wielding a giant piping bag. But when Rory had finally deemed a decorated cupcake perfect... Jack smiled. Proud didn't do what he'd felt at the time justice. He'd made a joke, embarrassed that a little cake had made him feel that way. *It's the icing on the cake,* he'd said with a self-conscious laugh, but Rory hadn't laughed. No, the icing on the cake was that Jack could now join him in the practical side of running the bakery; what their customers clamoured for, they could make *together*. They'd taken photographs of the cupcake before they'd shared it, taking a bite and a lick of the buttercream before they had taken a bite and a lick of each other. The memory was as sweet as the frosting, and Jack smiled as he piped.

One after the other, Jack topped the cupcakes with an expert swirl of deep golden buttercream. His world contracted to contain only him, a piping bag, and a tray of cakes. His hands were steady, and not one mistake was made. With a flourish, he piped up the last cupcake. Forty-eight perfect little specimens stood to attention in rows.

"They look lovely. Well done, Jack." Rory planted a soft kiss on Jack's cheek. "Now for the holly."

Rory took two boxes from the fridge. One contained little red icing balls to represent the berries, and in the other box were bright green leaves. The delicate pieces of icing were one of the very few things the bakery didn't produce itself. Rory bought them from a known and trusted supplier.

With a quick, and now expert hand, Jack placed two red berries in the centre of the frosting, and a green and shiny leaf on either side. This had been another job that had looked a lot easier than it was. His first few attempts had resulted in off-centre berries and wonky leaves smeared with bits of buttercream. It took a few goes to perfect the look, providing a another photo opportunity.

"I'll deliver these," Rory said as he packed up two boxes.

"Why? I normally do the deliveries.'

"Yes, but not when you've had a skinful of mulled wine, a bucket of snowball, and three large brandies the previous night." Rory's lips twitched in amusement.

Jack grunted. Rory was right, he supposed. "Last night, did we—?"

"Bunty was not harmed in the course of what may or may not have occurred."

Jack narrowed his eyes. Whatever they had done, he wished he could remember.

"Lance is due a break, so you'll need to work the counter with Mabel. You up to it, or do you need to have a little nap?" Rory grinned as he grabbed his coat from the office-staffroom.

Jack grunted. Whether he needed a nap or not, he wasn't going to get it.

With a quick kiss, Rory was gone, leaving Jack to take off his apron and paste a smile on his face to greet The Bakehouse's adoring public.

CHAPTER ELEVEN

"That woman, there. Do you see her, looking in through the window?" Mabel had no need to lower her voice. It was the rarest of times: The Bakehouse was empty of customers.

Jack followed the direction of her gaze. A woman, concentrating on the window display, was wrapped up in a heavy winter coat, a scarf, and a floppy woolly hat that disguised much of her face. She also wore a large pair of sunglasses. Okay, the winter sun was bright, but they seemed a little bit over the top for mid-December.

"What about her?" Jack asked.

"She's been hanging around for the past week or so, pretending to look at the display, but I know she's pretending because she keeps glancing at the counter. She's hesitated at the door a couple of times but never comes in. At first, I thought she hadn't seen anything she fancied, but when she came back the following day, I recognised her. Hard not to, wearing a stupid hat like that."

Mabel sniffed, and Jack glanced at her. Maybe he wouldn't mention her plastic cherry-adorned hat...

"What do you think she is? A spy? Is this some sort of clumsy industrial espionage? A rival baker, checking out the competition before they open up across the road? Will it be Danish at dawn, a muffin massacre?" Jack laughed as he began restocking the counter.

Mabel huffed. "All I'm saying is that I've noticed her do the same thing for over a week, now. If she wanted a cake or a loaf of bread, she would have come in, don't you think? There's something funny going on. You mark my words." Mabel folded her arms over her chest and nodded.

"Maybe she's on a diet, and is looking at all the things she knows she can't have."

Mabel's sigh was as dramatic as her carefully constructed beehive hairdo.

"No, Jack, she's not on a diet. If she were, she'd buy something and then eat it in secret. Secret scoffing doesn't count, because a *secret* cake doesn't have any calories. Don't you know anything?" Mabel tutted.

Jack looked up from restocking the front counter, towards the window. The woman, whoever she was, had gone. She must have lived or worked locally, somebody who passed the shop on her way to wherever, tempted by the goodies but knowing that they were not for her.

"If you see her again, you have my full permission to rush outside, rugby tackle her to the ground, and demand to know why she's staring at the goods but not buying."

Mabel opened her mouth to answer but the jangle of the door caught both their attention.

"Back again, sweetie? Did you forget something earlier? What can I do for you?" Mabel gave Mr. Art Supplies Shop a wide grin.

Russ, or Guss, answered with a tremulous smile and looked beyond Mabel to the partially open door that led to the back of the shop. His face had been hopeful when he walked in, but now he just looked scared.

"Lance is on a break at the moment, so you'll have to make do with me." Mabel's grin grew bigger.

The guy mumbled that he'd take half a dozen croissants and almost ran from the shop as soon as Mabel handed over the brown paper bag.

"Please don't alienate the customers." Jack put on his best HR director voice, but it would have little effect on his employee.

"I don't know what you mean." Mabel widened her eyes and looked at Jack with an angelic smile. "He *so* didn't come in for croissants. He was looking for Lance. I think it's really sweet, the way they both go as red as berries when they're within ten feet of each other. Who do you think will pluck up the courage to ask the other one out first? Perhaps I can help the course of true love along? I could be a matchmaker."

"No. Let them find their own—"

The door flew open, cutting off Jack's words of warning.

A group of women trooped in, all dressed in yoga gear. Jack glanced at his watch. One-thirty. That meant the lunchtime class at The Yoga Shack, a converted church a street or two away, had ended. The group nurtured their souls twice a week before they nurtured their sweet teeth straight after.

A couple of the women threw him lingering, pouty smiles. Jack's answering smile felt as stiff as a day-old baguette.

Why do they insist on flirting with me? They know I'm with Rory.

He kept his smile bright and bland, refusing to hold eye contact with the pushier, poutier women as he and Mabel worked the queue. At last they all left, carrying bagged-up sweet and savoury delights.

"Christ. Some of those women scare me half to death." Jack slumped against the counter.

Mabel laughed. "Only some? They're an okay

crowd, or mainly. Don't worry, you poor defenceless lad. As long as I'm here, you're safe."

Jack had no doubt about that at all. His smile felt pathetically grateful, and Mabel answered with a wink.

"Lance will be back soon, so why don't you head off to lunch?"

"Do you mind if I take an extra half hour? I need to have a chat with the manager at Sax Fiend. I'm part of a 1960s tribute Christmas gig, and I just want to go over a couple of details."

"Sure, no problem. Take whatever time you need. You really should be singing full-time, you know."

Jack meant every word. Mabel's voice was as rich and honeyed as the baklava Rory baked as a 'Special' one weekend a month.

"I used to think that, but I like doing different things. Keeps everything fresh. See you later."

The Bakehouse was rarely quiet, but the period that stretched from roughly from two to three o'clock in the afternoon was the exception. Alone in the shop, Jack's mind drifted as he carried out the tasks that had become second nature to him.

Rory always liked to open up alone at the start of the day. When Jack had said he'd come with him, he'd been gently rebuffed. Jack hadn't understood and had even been a little upset, but after he too had spent time alone in the shop, he'd come to understand. Yes, it was a different time of day, and outside, the little square was busy with people criss-crossing as they took a shortcut to the main road. But the quiet, the comforting sweet smells, the twinkling lights threaded along the counter, and the gently moving sparkly decorations made The Bakehouse magical.

Jack tidied the counter and rearranged the cakes on display to showcase them at their best. Not that they needed much showcasing, because Rory's skill was showcasing in itself.

His eyes fell to the Christmas pudding cupcakes he'd iced earlier. There were only two left. They had proved themselves to be a seasonal winner, and Jack liked to think that his newly acquired buttercream skills had had a big hand in that success. But it wasn't the case because it was Rory who was the driving force. With his talent, skill, and innate knowing what people wanted before they themselves even knew, Rory had to take the credit for the amazing success The Bakehouse was. And all in a year. Within three months, they had outstripped their initial income forecast. Business wasn't ticking over, it was galloping and showing no signs of slowing. Jack huffed out a laugh. And all because of cakes.

Jack planted his hands on his hips as he scrutinised the shop. The Bakehouse was long and thin, which was perfect if people were buying, then leaving, but if he and Rory were to add a café the shape was far from ideal. And a café would work, he knew in his bones it would.

He stared at the wall, but he didn't see the exposed brick or the mirror; he was seeing through it, to the soon-to-be-vacant shop next door. It was perfect. He had even made some enquiries, on the quiet. No, there had been little interest, and that was likely to remain the case until the spring, the commercial estate agent had told him. Expanding the bakehouse into a bakery-café had to be a no-brainer, but with Rory just about keeping a lid on his stress levels, it wasn't the time to make the suggestion. But... it would work, Jack knew it would.

His thoughts found the little place in Soho he'd been going to, on and off, for years. Barista Boys, that was his inspiration, but he and Rory could go further, he knew they could...

Jack flexed his shoulders. He needed to keep a rein on his ideas and pull them in, or at least for now. Ambition was a good thing, but he didn't want to scare Rory half to death with his still-forming plans for them to become the Kings of Cake. But, not so long ago, he'd had a long chat with Bernie, the owner of Barista Boys.

He'd done so on the quiet. Jack sucked on his bottom lip. He'd felt a bit bad, like he'd been going behind Rory's back, but didn't his fiancé have enough on his plate at the moment?

The chat with Bernie had been off the cuff and unplanned, as he'd called in on impulse for a fix of the best coffee in London when he'd been in the area. Bernie had taken him through to his office; the man had been inspirational, generous with his time, experience, and advice, and all in the busiest period of the day. If anybody could convince Rory it was the way to go, the gruff but friendly café owner was the one to do it.

Jack was so wrapped up in his thoughts it took a moment for him to realise he had a customer. Even the jangle of the door hadn't got through to him. He smiled but jerked back slightly when he saw who it was: the woman Mabel had pointed out to him earlier, the one who looked but never came in. But now she was here, when the shop was empty. Had she been waiting until there were no other customers?

"How can I help you?"

It was difficult to see what she looked like, so wrapped up in her winter clothes, the incongruous sunglasses still glued to her face.

For a moment she didn't say anything, just opened her mouth before shutting it again. Jack waited. Whatever it was she had come into The Bakehouse for, it wasn't a cupcake, a muffin, or a multigrain cobbler.

"Am I right in thinking Rory Kincaid works here?"

"May I ask why?"

The woman, short and slender from what Jack could make out, appeared harmless enough, but until he found out why she was asking, he wasn't giving anything away about Rory.

"I know him, or at least I did." The woman shifted her weight from one booted foot to the other.

It didn't seem like much of an answer, and Jack waited for more, saying nothing.

It was an old trick he'd picked up years before when he had worked in human resources. Don't fill the silence, let it hang, let the other person say things they never meant to. He always thought of it as being a cheap trick, but it was effective, and it came into its own now.

"It's been a long time since I last saw him. I thought, if he was here..."

The woman took off her sunglasses, clutching them tight as she looked beyond Jack towards the back of the shop, then back at Jack. She smiled, but there was nothing happy about it, only a kind of sadness and regret. She didn't say anything else.

Perhaps she needed a little prodding.

"My name's Jack, and Rory is my fiancé. If you

want to pass on a message, I'd be happy to take it for you."

The woman started; his words had shocked her into looking up at Jack with eyes wide with surprise.

"Oh, his fiancé? Really?" Her smile lit up, became easier, replacing the regretful sadness. She nodded as though pleased at the news. "So, you both work here, then?"

"We're the owners."

The woman's mouth opened and formed a perfect O of surprise.

"I'm pleased to see he's doing so well for himself and using his skills and talents to the full, I really and truly am."

She nodded again, as if confirming something to herself.

"If you tell me—"

"No, really, it's fine. He's doing well and is happy. And getting married. It's all I wanted to know."

She took a step backwards as she slipped her sunglasses back on.

"Please, if you give me your name, I can—"

The door crashed open and Lance rushed in, clutching a large parcel to his chest.

"Sorry I'm so late, Jack. I had to wait ages at the depot to pick this up. I couldn't leave it because I need it tonight." Lance's words tumbled out on a rush of breath as he dashed towards the back of the shop.

Jack turned back to the woman, but she had disappeared, leaving nothing behind to show that she had ever been there in the first place.

CHAPTER TWELVE

Sighing, Rory relaxed back into his seat. The coffee was rich, nutty, and scalding hot, just as he liked it.

He'd made the deliveries, battling through the stop-start West End traffic, and had left the little company van parked in the customer's tiny carpark. He needed a good coffee before the trek back to The Bakehouse.

Outside the customer's office, he'd looked up and down the street. No end of chain coffee shops... but then he'd remembered the little place he'd gone to with Jack, just a couple of days after they met, and a handful of times since. Less than five minutes later, he'd pushed open the door of the Soho café.

Rory bit into the slice of lemon meringue pie he'd bought to go with his coffee, closed his eyes, and groaned. It was delicious. Crisp, sweet pastry, then a generous layer of dense lemon curd, sharp without being tart, and topped with light-as-air meringue. It was a triumph, and Rory wanted it in The Bakehouse *now*.

Opening his eyes, Rory studied the busy café from his corner seat.

Like The Bakehouse, a never-ending stream of customers waited to be served. But Barista Boys was a café rather than a bakery, although the range of baked goods on offer was almost as extensive as those in The Bakehouse.

Through the steam rising from his mug, Rory was almost painfully aware of everything going on around him.

A year ago, he would have looked at the scene and just seen a busy and popular café. Now, he looked at what was happening through the eyes of a businessman. Every single one of the tables was occupied, with Christmas shoppers taking a break and filling up on extravagant coffees, hot chocolates, and sweet and savoury pies, tarts, and muffins. Plus, there was the takeaway trade, as people handed over their refillable coffee mugs and picked up freshly made sandwiches and cakes.

It wasn't just the quality of the product on offer — and Barista Boys was top notch — it was how the staff interacted with the customers that created repeat business. That many were regulars was easy to see. The baristas kept up a steady flow of banter with those they served. Was this the kind of place he wanted for him and Jack? Possibly, maybe. But it would mean expanding, perhaps into the shop next door, which would soon become vacant. Rory blew out a long breath. It was a lot to think about, too much with everything else going on around them, but he had to look forward, he had to think of their future.

Jack was already doing just that.

Rory smiled. He'd seen Jack eyeing the shop next door to them, and the look of concentration in his fiancé's narrowed eyes and puckered brow. Oh yes, he had already guessed what Jack was thinking... *But aren't I thinking the same thing?* Absorbing everything that was happening around him, he knew what was possible. Yes, they needed a conversation, but as Rory closed his eyes once more and took another sip of coffee, in that moment what he wanted more than anything was just some time by himself and for himself.

The vibration against his hip from his mobile phone told him loud and clear that that was *not* what he was going to be getting.

Rory's heart fell when he saw the name displayed on his phone. Diana. Maybe this time she really did want to speak to him about ribbons. He was tempted to send the call to voicemail, but that would only be putting off the inevitable. He pressed accept and took a deep breath.

"Hi, Diana," he said, injecting a cheeriness into his voice he wasn't feeling.

His greeting was met with a throaty chuckle.

"It's your lucky day. I bet you were tempted to send the call to voicemail. You were, weren't you?"

Rory laughed as relief loosened his muscles. *No bloody ribbons...*

"Why are you using your mum's phone?"

"Mine's on charge, so I grabbed hers," Caroline, Rory's soon-to-be sister-in-law, answered. "Sorry if I gave you a fright." Her voice bubbled over with laughter.

"You didn't. Your mum doesn't frighten me. Or not much."

Caroline's 'hmm' was noncommittal.

"Is she being a pain in the arse over the wedding preparations? She was like a raging inferno when I got married. Impossible to resist. I know what it's like."

Rory took his time to answer. "I appreciate everything she's doing because I'd have no idea, but—"

"No need to be diplomatic with me. You feel like it's all been taken out of your hands. I understand, honestly I do, but the only thing I will say is that come the day, you'll see what a fantastic job she'll have done and all the pain will have been worth it. She really does know what she's doing, Rory, when it comes to this sort of thing."

Rory stifled a groan. *Which only makes me feel all the worse.*

"I'm spending a couple of days in London, here at the house," she said, referring to the De Lacys' London home in Chelsea. "I'm combining some Christmas shopping with my final fitting."

Bespoke tailoring and dressmaking... The sums being spent on his and Jack's so-called simple wedding were eye-watering. His own upbringing had been very humble, and when he had found himself on the streets, every pound, every *penny*, went towards just staying alive.

"... what?"

Rory hadn't heard a word she had said.

"I said, I called Jack, and he told me you were out and about delivering in the West End. He suggested I call you to see if you wanted a catch-up. Not that I wouldn't have done that in any case." Caroline paused. "He mentioned the other evening, when Mum came to visit, and the sudden expansion of the guest list."

"What did he say? That I'm a neurotic, ungrateful mess? He wouldn't be far off the truth."

"Rory, he said nothing of the sort. And you were perfectly entitled to be less than pleased with her. She should have spoken to you both first. It's as simple as that."

Rory sighed. "I'm sorry, Caroline. I didn't mean to bitch."

"Of course you meant to bitch, and I don't blame you. We're dealing with *Mother*, don't forget. Jack does understand how much you're feeling the pressure of the wedding, you know," Caroline added, her voice softening.

"I know. He's handling it all better than I am."

"So off-load on him more. He can take it, and would want to. Don't forget that taking a bit of time out is important, a good stress reliever. Plus, you've got a pass to play hooky, don't forget. We could meet for lunch or just coffee?"

Warmth bubbled through him. Jack had known what he'd needed more than he had himself. Time out, with a good friend, because that was what Caroline was. He smiled to himself.

"That would be great."

They agreed Caroline would join him in the café, and when she arrived, Rory greeted her with a warm, hard hug.

"My dress and hat will be delivered to Chelsea in the next couple of days, but I was able to pick up my shoes today," she said, holding up and waggling a bag containing a shoebox.

Rory wondered if the shoes, too, had been handmade. Probably, but he wasn't going to ask.

"I swear Dad went ghost white when he saw the dressmaker's bill." Caroline laughed as she settled herself down at the table. "He owed me for stepping in and co-hosting a dinner for the sheep division of the regional Young Farmers' when Mum was ill with the flu. You can imagine how exciting *that* evening was. Honestly, I haven't been able to look a lamb chop in the face since." She gave Rory a wide-mouthed smile, her bright blue eyes twinkling.

Rory shook his head. She would have charmed them all.

Caroline insisted on buying lunch, and despite the lemon meringue and coffee, Rory was happy to dive into a toasted sandwich, another coffee, and a muffin.

"It's for research purposes," he said, doing his best to adopt a deadpan expression. And it was partly true. Barista Boys was doing a very brisk trade, and he had noticed the white chocolate and cranberry muffins flying off the shelf.

"Getting ideas to add to the range?" Caroline asked when a young café employee with soft auburn hair and a lightbulb-bright smile brought over a laden tray.

"Kind of. It doesn't hurt to see what others are doing, especially when they're doing it very well. Like here."

"This is really good," Caroline said, after they'd spent a couple of minutes in silence as they'd tucked in. "But I'm sure you would do even better once you've set your mind to it." She sat back and took a sip of her latte, closed her eyes, and sighed in contentment.

Rory smiled. She was doing exactly what he had been just an hour before.

Caroline snapped her eyes open, all coffee-and-carb-induced dreaminess gone. She wasn't looking at him, she was scrutinising him. He knew that look because it was the same one Jack had when he was thinking hard. The slight narrowing of the eyes, and the slighter puckering of the brow. He waited for what she had to say, and he didn't have to wait long.

"You're looking very tired, if I might say so."

Rory shrugged. "Your mum said the same. But it's to be expected because we're extremely busy. I really shouldn't be here, I suppose, as there's so much to do back at the bakery. I'm not afraid of hard work, but sometimes I feel deluged by it all."

Rory stirred his coffee, avoiding Caroline's eye.

"Talking helps, you know, especially when I suspect you're not really talking about the bakery," she said with a crooked smile.

Rory huffed. Another De Lacy who had the knack of seeing through him.

"I've been through it, too, don't forget."

It. A De Lacy wedding.

Rory let his spoon clatter onto the table as he sat back and met Caroline's steady gaze.

"Sometimes, I wish we'd gone off somewhere and got married on the beach and then come home and told everyone. Just me and Jack, and no fuss. And that makes me feel really, really guilty. You must think I'm an ungrateful little shit." He hadn't meant to blurt to Caroline, but it had come tumbling out before he could bite the words back.

"Believe me, I completely understand, especially when you're being asked for your opinion on which shade of cream the table linen should be, as though the future of humanity depended upon it, when you don't give damn. Honestly, all the details which seem so pointless can be overwhelming, and it feels as though it gets worse as the day draws closer."

"We were talking about flower arrangements for the tables, the other night." Rory's lips curved up in a wan smile.

"Oh, I remember those conversations. Several of them. You've done well if you've got away with only the one. But it's not just the deluge of practical arrangements, and Mother Dearest's talk of roses and orchids, is it? There's more going on, I can tell. I've bought you lunch, after all, so you can't *not* tell me."

Rory huffed out a small laugh. But how could he

explain to Caroline when he could barely explain to himself?

"What is it, Rory? Really?" Caroline's voice was low, inviting confidence, as she laid a warm hand on the back of his.

Rory swallowed. He'd try and explain, and no doubt make a pig's ear of it. Would she think he was being silly or that it was just a case of pre-wedding jitters? He took a deep breath.

"Sometimes, I just don't feel good enough. For Jack, or the family."

Silence sat heavy and bloated between them.

"Oh, Rory. No, no, *no*. That's not the case. Why do you even think such a thing? All that matters to any of us is that you and Jack are happy. And you are, any fool can see that. It doesn't matter who you are or where you come from—"

"It's easy for you to say that. You've got all this tradition and history behind you and the confidence it brings. I don't have any of that. I have no idea who my natural parents are, and my adoptive ones ended up not giving a damn about me."

Caroline squeezed his hand tight.

"We're just a family, Rory, when it comes down to it. Mum and Dad might be Lady Diana and Sir Roger, but first and foremost they're parents, and they'd be the first to admit it. And they're good parents, which means all that matters for them is that their children are happy, with whomever it is they happen to fall in love with. And that means you, Rory. *You*. Don't let all the trappings distract you. You and Jack are made for each other, it's as clear as daylight and everybody can see it. Maybe you need to take a step back to remind yourself of that."

"Jack's everything I've ever wanted—"

"And you're everything he's ever wanted, and it didn't take him long to find out," she said with a smile.

It was true. Within days of the chance encounter that had brought them into each other's lives, all their surface differences had been swept away as they'd fallen in love in the depth of a snowy winter.

"If it helps in any way, Tim had some of the same thoughts as you, to the extent that we almost called the wedding off. Nobody else knows that, by the way."

"What? You almost didn't go through with it?"

Rory gaped at Caroline.

"It's difficult to credit, isn't it? But the nearer we got to the day, Tim really did start to struggle with the *marrying a De Lacy* codswallop. His fears weren't so different to yours, but they were unfounded and came to nothing in the end, just as yours will.'

"God, I don't know what to say. I can't imagine you and Tim not being together."

"Nor could we, even though our backgrounds had

nothing in common. His mother worked part-time as a nurse, and his dad was the manager at a pet food supplies company in Birmingham." She shrugged. "Tim doesn't come from the aristocracy, major, minor, or anything in between. His parents are ordinary people who'd always worked hard to provide for Tim and his brother. Yet he couldn't help thinking none of it worked in his favour, because in moments of panic — and when our wedding was looming those moments were coming thick and fast, believe me — all he saw were the trappings and not the substance. But he was so wrong, as are you, if I might say.

"The one thing my parents admire more than anything is commitment, a sense of purpose, and hard work because they are virtues they possess. Mum and Dad have worked tirelessly to make the estate the success it is. They saw that same commitment in Tim in the way he built up his vets practice, and I know they feel exactly the same about you and the bakery and the huge success you and Jack are together. The two of you are a partnership, and they're immensely proud of that."

"That I've risen above my humble origins, you mean?" Rory said, a wry smile lifting his lips.

"Yes, something like that. Much like Tim," she said with a short laugh. "But seriously. The only thing my parents are interested in is their children's happiness.

You make Jack happy, and in the end that's all that matters." Caroline gave his hand a final, hard squeeze, letting go to sit back in her chair.

They let the subject drop. Caroline launched into the latest gossip and the carryings-on in Polton Lacy, making Rory laugh with tales of the deadly rivalry between the Polton Lacy Ladies' Guild and the Friends of St Peter's church for who could provide the best and most elaborate stall at the village's Christmas fair.

"Honestly," Caroline said, as she got up to go. "Rural life is a minefield of seething jealousy, personal antagonism, and feuds. The worst of all are the sweet-faced, smiling old grannies who fool you into thinking they spend all their time making strawberry jam, baking fruitcakes, and arranging flowers in between doing good works. If looks could kill and tittle-tattle were offensive weapons, there would be nobody left in villages like Polton Lacy up and down the country. You don't know how easy you have it here in the city."

Rory laughed. Village life in all its intensity, city living was a piece of cake in comparison.

"Please don't let everything become overwhelming. Just focus on that moment when you and Jack exchange your vows, when you become husbands. That's all that matters. Everything else is mere decoration. But if you want to talk or scream in frustration, you know where I am. I must dash as I'm meeting old friends later, and then getting the early train back in the morning."

Out on the street, they shared a long, hard hug before Caroline set off in one direction and Rory in another.

CHAPTER THIRTEEN

The hectic day had rushed them off their feet. At last, the torrent of customers turned to a trickle then dried up as the working day drew to a close. Rory flexed his aching shoulders and twisted his neck from side to side. A lazy evening consisting of a hot bath, dinner, the TV, and falling asleep on Jack awaited him. He sniggered to himself; life really was rock 'n' roll.

With less than half an hour to go until closing, Mabel was clearing the counter so that it was ready for restocking first thing in the morning, while Lance swept the floor. When Jack had left about an hour before to make some local deliveries, he'd whispered in his ear that by the time Rory got home, he'd have something hot and tasty ready and waiting. Rory smiled to himself. The only hot and tasty he was looking forward to that night was the chicken stew bubbling away in the slow cooker.

Rory glanced through the window, and his eyes widened in surprise. The on-off wet sleet had turned to snow and was falling in thick, feathery flakes; it had already settled on the pavement and was starting to bank up on the windows. He glanced at his employees. Neither had far to go, but he didn't want to keep them at The Bakehouse longer than necessary.

"Lance, don't worry about that. I'll sweep up and give the floor a wash. Head off home before it gets worse. You too, Mabel."

With a grateful smile, Lance dashed off to pull on his coat and gloves and, with a wave, was on his way.

"I won't argue," Mabel said. "I'm helping out with the Christmas carol concert at an old folks' home later on. There's a group of us singing a cappella-style favourite carols, but we're doing a few Motown numbers, too." With a wide smile, Mabel too was gone, leaving Rory alone in the bakery.

The snow began falling heavier than ever. Nobody was going to come in now, especially with no more than fifteen minutes to go until they officially closed.

I'll just finish sweeping the floor...

The door jangled as it opened, and Rory looked up, a smile ready and waiting. The last customer of the day.

The smile froze on his lips, and the broom clattered to the floor as it slipped from his hands.

The woman he had never expected to see again stood before him.

It didn't matter that she was wrapped in a heavy winter coat; it didn't matter that a thick, soft-looking scarf wound its way around her neck; it didn't matter that she had a matching floppy woollen hat pulled low over her head. None of it mattered, because he would have recognised Sonia Kincaid, his adoptive mother, anywhere.

Rory stared and blinked, and carried on staring, unable to speak, his tongue taken captive by shock.

"Rory?"

His name on her lips, not heard for years, jolted him out of his paralysis.

"Sonia." It was all he could croak.

She was the same but different. *Had she really been so short?*

Sonia, he could tell, was slimmer, even under the heavy winter clothes. The coat and accessories, they were good, giving her a style he couldn't remember her possessing before. Tufts of hair, soft blonde rather than the mousy brown he'd always known, poked out from under the hat. Whatever had happened to Sonia Kincaid, she was no longer the dowdy, harried woman whose affection for him during his childhood and teenage years had been little more than tepid.

"I know I'm probably the last person you ever wanted to see again."

Her shoulders slouched, and her lips twisted in a sad smile, but with a sudden and unexpected pierce to his heart, there was a softness in her eyes Rory couldn't recall ever seeing before.

"If you told me to go, I'd honestly understand. But when I realised it was you who worked here, it wouldn't leave me alone."

"What wouldn't?" Rory's voice was rough and rasping, his mouth dry, and he licked his lips.

"The need to come and say sorry."

I don't want or need you in my life... I'm happier than I've ever been... I have a man who loves me... I've made a success of my life, and all of this I've achieved without you...

All the words he wanted to say; all the words he couldn't as he stood and stared, the dropped broom lying between them like a border neither dared to cross.

Standing just feet away from her, Rory didn't know *what* he wanted to say to Sonia, but neither did she, judging by the way she shifted her weight from foot to foot and wrangled her hands together.

Sonia broke the heavy silence.

"I'm sorry. I shouldn't have come. You've found a new life for yourself, and I don't blame you if you don't want any reminder of your old one. I just want you to know I'm so, so sorry I was never the mum you wanted or deserved. It took me too long to realise it. Far too long. I wish you well, Rory, I honestly do, and," she said, glancing around The Bakehouse and smiling, "it's good to know that everything's turned out right for you. I'll go now. I just wanted to..." Sonia shrugged, the sad, regretful smile once more curving her lips down, as she turned to leave.

"No." The word was loud and hard. "No. Please, don't go." The words tumbled from Rory's lips as the all-encompassing and overwhelming need to know what had happened to the people who had once been his family broke like a wave over his head. "I think we should talk."

Sonia answered with a tremulous smile and a small nod.

Rory rushed to the door, threw the lock, and turned the sign that declared they were closed for the day.

"I'll make some coffee, and perhaps you would like..." He motioned towards the counter where some stock remained, ready to be covered over to be sold the following day. He plated up a muffin and took it into the staff kitchen area, with Sonia on his heels.

With mugs of steaming coffee before them, they sat

across from one another at the tiny table. Rory clutched at his drink, barely heeding its scalding heat. Where to start, what to say, he had no idea. Sonia solved it for him.

"Peter and I divorced almost three years ago."

"Oh. I'm sorry." *Am I?*

Sonia shrugged. "Don't be, because I'm not. Our marriage had been under strain for years, and it only got worse with the unexpected arrival of the twins."

The twins. The spoilt, vicious little girls to whom Rory had always tried to be a big brother.

"They're better than they were. So much better. They were horrible kids." Sonia shook her head. "That's not something you're supposed to say about your children, but that's what they were. And it was all our fault, mine and Peter's. We spoilt them and let them run riot. But you wouldn't recognise them now. They're decent, polite girls who are doing well in school. I know how hard that must be for you to believe."

Rory shrugged. Who and what the girls were now was of no consequence. It didn't matter, but there were questions that did. He took another sip of coffee before he spoke.

"How did you find me here?"

Sonia had taken her hat and scarf off, and she pushed the blonde hair Rory didn't remember away from her brow as she golf balled her cheeks and exhaled a long breath.

"It was pure chance. When Peter and I divorced, I had to get myself a job, and fast. But it was difficult, having been out of the workplace for so long. So I became a full-time temp. A few weeks here, a few months there, that kind of thing. My last temp job wasn't too far from here and finished last week, but a month ago I had to go somewhere after work. I cut across the square, and I saw you, getting out of your delivery van and coming in here. I—I hid. I dashed into the little garden outside."

"You — hid?"

Rory stared at her, watched the flush creep up her face.

"It was stupid, but I was scared. I didn't know what you'd say if I approached you, returning like some horrible ghost from the past. But I couldn't just leave it. So I kept coming back, never quite plucking up the courage to come in, but I think that young woman who works here spotted me."

"Mabel," Rory said automatically. Why *wouldn't* she have been scared? A child she had never been more than indifferent to was now a man. *He* was that man. What welcome did she think she'd receive, if any?

Rory studied the woman, holding tight to her

coffee mug as though her life depended on it, who had once been his mother.

I have every right to tell her to go, to push her away with as little thought as she did to me... But as he looked at her across the other side of the small table, Rory couldn't do it because more than anything, he wanted to know what had happened to this woman who was as much a stranger as she was known.

"I was scared of what I might see in your eyes. You always wore your heart on your sleeve, you could never hide what you were feeling. I imagined all sorts of scenarios. Loathing and anger, but the worst was disinterest. So I've been a coward, lurking outside, peering in through the window but never summoning up the courage to come in."

"Until today," Rory said.

"Not exactly."

Rory sat up straighter. "What do you mean?"

"Oh. I thought he, your fiancé I mean, would have told you. I came in, a couple of days back. But I didn't tell him who I was, so maybe he didn't think it was worth mentioning."

Rory stared at her. She'd already come into the shop? She'd *spoken to Jack?*

Then why the hell didn't he...?

Rory rubbed one hand down his face, exhaling hard. It wasn't Jack's fault; he couldn't be blamed for not realising the random stranger was the adoptive mother who'd long since faded from Rory's life. There was no reason for Jack to have made the connection. He'd never shown Jack any photos of Sonia because he had none to show; yet even if he had, she was unrecognisable as the woman she'd once been.

"... today, because it's my last chance, you see."

"Sorry? What's your last chance?'

"I'm leaving. Starting a new life abroad."

"You're going away?" *Why should I care?* He shouldn't, he had no reason to, so why did her words feel like a shove in the chest? Why was she leaving when she'd only just found him?

"I'm leaving for southern Spain, the day after tomorrow. Because I've met somebody.'

"Oh. That's good."

Sonia nodded, her face lighting up in a bright, joyous smile. It was something else Rory didn't recognise about her.

"After Peter left, my life was a mess. He provided no financial or emotional support to help with the twins, and their bad behaviour just got worse. I was at my wits' end. One evening I had to get out of the house. I was crying, and I literally bumped into my new neighbour. He asked me what the problem was, and it all came tumbling out. Well, that was Bobby, the chap I'm now with.

"From that moment, everything changed. He's a widower, with two girls of his own, older than the twins, more your age. The girls responded to him in a way they never did to Peter. One look, or the right word, and it was enough to stop them in their tracks. Bobby wasn't only the best thing to happen to me, he was the best thing to happen to the girls. They adore him, and they've changed because of his good influence. And I like to think I've changed, too."

Sonia took a sip of coffee and a bite of her muffin.

"This is delicious, but you always were the best cook in the house." She said the words with a light laugh, but it fell away as a shadow passed over her face.

"I tried to find you." She spoke quietly, staring down into her coffee as she rolled pieces of muffin crumb, forming little tight balls of chocolate sponge. "It was Bobby. He persuaded me to try. He said I needed to make amends, and that I owed you an apology for not being the mother I should've been. They were hard words to listen to because I knew they were true. And I did try to find you, Rory. I went to your flat, the last address I had, the one you shared with—"

"Adrian."

His ex. The man he had gone to live with just so he could escape his life with the Kincaids. Adrian, another name from a past he didn't want to revisit.

Sonia nodded. "But you weren't there, and that

restaurant you worked at was gone, turned into flats or something. I searched on social media, on Facebook and so on, but came up with nothing. I tried, I honestly did. I even got in touch with Peter, though by that time, we were barely talking, but he had no information he could give me."

"Well, you've found me now."

Rory didn't know what else to say. The woman in front of him seemed genuinely contrite. *But do I really, honestly care?* Sonia was part of a dim and distant life, a life that often felt like it had happened to somebody else.

But it had happened to *him*.

The words he uttered felt like they were being torn from his heart.

"I tried my hardest, Sonia. I tried to be a good son, and I tried to be a good brother to the twins, but everything I did, it was never good enough. You and Peter made me feel worthless. It was why I left home, latching on to the first person who showed an interest in me."

What was the point in sugaring the pill? Sonia and Peter had been bad parents. Why should he pretend they hadn't been?

"We were lousy parents. I see that now. But when the twins came along, they were so demanding, and you were always quietly self-sufficient, or that's what I thought. But it's no excuse. I can't mend the past Rory. I wish I could. All I can say is how sorry I am."

What could he say? She couldn't put right what had happened, neither of them could. But the present? The future? Did he want those to be as broken as the past? But she was leaving.

"Why are you going to Spain?"

Her smile outshone the light hanging from the ceiling.

"Bobby's got a bar out there. His retirement project, he calls it. It's a typical expat type of place, and that's where we're going to make our new life. I stayed behind to kind of pack up our life, but now it's time to go. I'll be coming back from time to time, as I've still got good friends here."

She hesitated, and Rory waited for her next words.

"And when I come back, I'd like to see you. If you would like that, too? If you don't, I understand, but now that I found you, I don't want to lose you again."

It would be so easy to say no, to put Sonia and everything to do with his life with the Kincaids aside.

"Yes. I—I'd like that. To see you again, and keep in touch." The words he thought he would never say to Sonia Kincaid.

"Thank you," she said quietly. "The weather, it's getting worse. That's one thing I won't miss." She nodded towards the window that looked out over the tiny backyard. It was filled with whiteness, the snow banked up on the sill outside, falling thicker and heavier than ever.

Rory glanced up at the battered wall clock, surprised to see over an hour had passed since he'd led Sonia into the little room. Jack would be home, and if he didn't contact him soon, he'd be getting worried.

He led Sonia out through the bakery to the shop door. She smiled as she looked around at the mismatched, eclectic decorations, and the twinkling tree in the window, laughing when her gaze settled upon Doris, the drag queen Christmas fairy. Rory smiled. Sonia's laugh was lighter and more carefree than he ever remembered it. And he was glad.

"Your fiancé—"

"Jack."

Sonia smiled. "I only spoke to him briefly, but he was nice. And very well spoken. Handsome, too." Her smile widened.

"He is, on all counts. Jack's the best thing to have happened to me."

Should he tell her how they'd met? About this wretched life on the streets before Jack found him huddled on his porch on a night so much like the freezing, snowy one on the other side of the door? No. There was no point. It was in the past, like so much else.

"When are you getting married?"

"Christmas Eve."

"Oh! That's just... Goodness, so soon. I'll be in Spain, starting a new life just as you start yours." She paused, and a small, wistful smile lifted her lips. "I wish you all the best, Rory, with all the happiness and all the love you deserve. I'll be thinking of you on the day, I promise."

Emails were exchanged, along with an address of a house and a bar in a seaside town in Andalusia, scribbled on a scrap of paper and handed over.

They didn't hug. They didn't kiss. There was no long drawn-out goodbye. In many ways they were strangers, but as he watched the woman who had been his mother fade into the swirling snowstorm, he didn't want Sonia Kincaid to fade from his life a second time.

CHAPTER FOURTEEN

The front door slammed closed. Seconds later Rory, his winter hat and coat dusted with melting snow, walked into the living room. He closed the door and fell back against it with a thud.

"Hey, I was just about to call you. I was starting to get worried, especially now the weather's turned."

When Rory didn't answer, Jack peered at his fiancé.

"Ro? Are you okay? Were there problems at the shop?"

Rory's answer was a shake of his head, yet something had happened, Jack saw it in the dazed confusion in his eyes. A handful of steps and he was in front of Rory, cupping his fiancé's cold face between his palms.

"You look like you've seen a ghost. What the hell's

happened? And don't say nothing because I wouldn't believe you."

"A ghost? You could say that."

Jack's hands fell away as Rory pushed himself from the door, took his hat and coat off, and dropped them on a nearby chair.

"Then what...?"

"I was in the shop on my own. I let Mabel and Lance go early, and—"

"What?"

Jack's hand flew to his mobile, buried in the pocket of his jeans. He dragged it out, ready to call the police. Had somebody gone into the shop, seeing Rory alone? Had they threatened him? Stolen the takings? He couldn't give a damn about the money in the till, it was Rory that mattered—

"Jack." Rory closed his hands around Jack's, stopping him from making the emergency call. "Whatever you're thinking, stop it. Everything's fine at the shop and with me. I'm just a bit shell shocked, that's all."

"You're going to have to tell me what the hell's happened. I'm not getting it." Jack stuffed his phone back into his pocket with an unsteady hand.

"I'm not sure I am." Rory flopped down onto the sofa, and Jack sat next to him.

Rory sucked on his lower lip. His brow was gently

furrowed. It was a look of both concentration and confusion.

"Ro?"

"Sonia came into the shop."

For a moment Jack was confused. Who the hell was—? And then it crashed down on him. Sonia. Sonia Kincaid, the woman who called herself Rory's mother, the woman who'd been happy to see Rory walk out of her life.

"Fucking hell. Jesus. That must have been—I don't know how that must have been."

"Yeah." Rory stared into the fire, his brow puckered in thought. "I mean, it was a shock, but I'm okay. Which is a bit weird in itself," he said with a shrug as he turned his gaze to Jack. "You met her in the week. She came into the bakery, asking about me."

"What?"

Jack gazed into Rory's steady eyes as realisation hit him.

Oh, God... A middle-aged woman, looking for Rory, the so-called mother who'd washed her hands of her son. He should have realised, he should have known.

He should have thrown her out of the shop.

Rory snuggled into his side and slid his arms around Jack's middle.

"I don't think it's a cuddle I deserve. I should have put two and two together and warned you. Warned her to keep away." Jack slipped his arms around Rory and pulled him in tight. He didn't deserve Rory's hug, but he'd take one from him any day, and give one in return.

"I think I need to breathe, Jack." Light laughter rippled through Rory's voice, and Jack released his vice-like hold with reluctance. "It's as well you didn't twig who she was because I'm glad we had the chance to talk. That wouldn't have happened if you'd got all over-protective."

"How can you be glad about it? I don't understand."

Rory sat up and hunched forward, elbows on knees, as he stared into the fire. Jack rubbed his back in slow, wide circles, letting Rory know he was there for him, waiting for his fiancé to gather his thoughts.

"She's different to how she was before. Softer, less brittle," Rory said slowly. "I recognised her, but at the same time I didn't. I certainly didn't think of her as my mother."

"She had no right to come anywhere near you. The woman washed her hands of you." Jack ground the words out.

Why wasn't Rory angry or upset? Why didn't he accept that she had no right to even breathe the same air as he did? He didn't understand. His own parents flashed through his mind. A mother who was a force of nature and a quiet but strong-willed father, love and support had been lavished on him, Caroline, and George from the day they had entered the world. He'd grown up thinking all parents were like his, but it had been Rory's sad experience that had shown him how wrong he'd been.

"Yes, she did, but I'm glad she had the courage to come into the shop."

"What? What courage did she show?" Jack jumped up from the sofa. He paced the living room, too small to contain his burning anger. Rory wasn't angry when he had every cause to be, but he had anger enough for both of them.

"Jack, please. Come and sit down."

Jack stopped his pacing and stared down into Rory's upturned face. The dazed confusion of earlier was gone; instead, Rory gazed up at him through clear, calm eyes. But there was something else there, too, and with a jolt, Jack saw what it was: contentment, as though something had been resolved. He sank back down onto the sofa, and Rory took hold of his hands, his touch instantly calming and soothing as he swept his thumbs over Jack's knuckles. The steady backwards and forwards movement, its aim to still, quiet, and calm.

"Yes, I do think she was courageous because she didn't know what sort of reception she would get from me. She probably thought I'd be angry and tell her to go."

"And you would've had every right to do that," Jack grumbled.

"I would have, but what would've been the point? She's on the cusp of a new life herself and is happier and more content than the woman I remember. Why should I begrudge her that?"

Jack had a hundred and one reasons why, but he bit them back. It was one of the things he loved so much about Rory. His compassion, his understanding, his willingness not to hold grudges; instead, he showed, through his thoughts and actions, his innate desire to do the right thing and live in harmony with those who came into his life. It was little short of a miracle he retained his faith in people when so many bad things had happened to him, and so much had been thrown at him. *But...*

"But she was your mother, Ro. She should've been there for you, giving you the support you needed." *She should've loved you more.*

Rory nodded. "You're right, but I can't change the past. All I can do is try and make sure the future is better and brighter. She gave me her address and other contact details."

Rory pulled the scrap of paper from the pocket of his jeans and held it up.

"It was her last chance to speak to me because she's flying out to Spain to start a new life, but she wants us to keep in touch, and I want that, too. Oh, Jack, I know it's difficult for you to understand because you've got a tight-knit and loving family all around you. You've always had that, and I think you take it for granted. I don't blame you."

"What do you mean?" But Jack knew, deep down. Through his anger and indignation, he was beginning to understand why Rory hadn't told Sonia to go. She was a link to his past, evidence that he wasn't a rootless orphan.

Do I take my own family for granted? He'd never thought about it because he'd never had to. They were there, as solid and firm as the ground beneath his feet. Rory's family life had been like quicksand. Rather than drown, he'd reached out to the first person who'd shown him any kind of love, or even interest. But the safety and stability he craved had been nothing more than an illusion, when he'd found himself betrayed and abandoned.

"I feel as though something's been resolved. It's like the epilogue of a book, I suppose. All loose ends tied up, and looking forward to something better."

Rory stared down at their joined hands. Jack studied him in the warm, flickering lights, and waited for the words he knew Rory would say

"I could never think of Sonia as my mother again. Too much has happened. But now I've been given the chance of some kind of relationship with her, I'd like to make it work, even if it is just an occasional email. You probably think I'm a fool." Rory quirked his brow, almost daring Jack to answer.

"Not a fool, but a loving, generous-hearted, and good man. I'm not sure I could be quite so noble if our positions were reversed, but if you want to keep some form of contact, then I'll support you all the way. You know I will."

"I'm not being noble. I'm being selfish. This is about me and what I want, and what I want right now is for you to kiss me." Rory smiled, and Jack's heart melted, just like it did every time Rory looked at him.

Jack enveloped him in his arms, pulling him tight into his body. Kisses, lots and lots of kisses, light and comforting rather than hot and needy. This was a time for holding Rory close. To comfort, to make him feel safe, protected, and wanted; it was what Rory craved, so it was what Rory got. It was as simple as breathing.

Rory sighed and snuggled into Jack. They lay on the sofa, twisted, entwined, and knotted around each other. The only sounds were their steady breathing and the crackle from the wood burning stove.

Jack sifted his fingers through Rory's thick, dark hair. Soft and silky, he would never get tired of the feel of it running through his hands. He glanced down, not surprised to see his fiancé had fallen asleep. A business to run, the wedding, and now a face from the past Rory wanted to take into the future. Jack smiled. No wonder his man was exhausted.

"I love you, Rory Kincaid. I love you for being you. I love you for being the good and decent man you are." Jack whispered the words before he shifted to ease himself out from under Rory, who sighed and muttered in his sleep.

Gently, carefully, knowing he was holding the most precious cargo in the entire world, Jack hooked his arms under Rory's knees and around the top of his back, and lifted. Rory didn't stir, taking refuge from a world that was demanding so much from him.

Jack held the greatest treasure any man could have, as he took the man he loved so much through to the bedroom to lay him down to rest.

CHAPTER FIFTEEN

"Perfect, absolutely perfect. Wouldn't you agree, Cecil?" The short man with the wispy hair and beatific smile turned to an even shorter but equally wispy-headed man next to him.

"Yes, Cedric. I think our work here is done."

Cecil's smile was as angelic as his brother's. Both men wore identical suits and had tape measures dangling around their necks as they rested their hands on their identical paunches. Rory tried to smile back, but it was stiff and forced. Cecil and Cedric Bonville, bespoke tailors, were always smiling. Their round, beady button eyes sent a chill down Rory's backbone, making him think of Victorian china dolls, the kind that always seemed to crop up in horror films. Cecil and Cedric tilted their heads to the left, then to the right, in perfect time to each other, as they studied Rory, their smiles fixed and unwavering.

The tailor's shop was tucked into a little road at the back of Saville Row, the epicentre of high-class bespoke tailoring in London. The Bonville family had been making suits for the De Lacy men, and for those who were about to come into the family, for over two hundred years. It was the final fitting, just three days before the wedding, and the suit would be delivered to Jack's parents' house the following morning, to join the shoes and handmade shirt ready and waiting for him on Christmas Eve.

Jack's fitting had taken place before his, and he was in the little waiting area away from the changing room. Their suits were identical, but neither had wanted to see the other in them before their wedding day. It was a bit silly, Rory supposed, because theirs wasn't a traditional wedding.

Sometimes he had to pinch himself to believe that he and Jack had the freedom to get married at all. Equal marriage was still a new thing and was evolving, creating its own traditions distinct from that of the marriage between a man and a woman. Yet they had claimed one age-old tradition, and that was to not see each other in their wedding clothes before the day they spoke their vows to each other.

"Would Sir care to...?" One of the Bonville brothers, and Rory wasn't sure if it was Cecil or Cedric, indicated the full-length mirror.

Rory shook his head, and the brothers accepted his decision with another of their creepy smiles. It was the same procedure every time: Cecil or Cedric invited him to look in the mirror, and Rory declined. When he had confessed his odd little decision to Jack, shyness had crept over him, sure Jack would think he was being silly. Jack had only smiled, and confessed that he too had told the tailors the same thing.

The brothers helped Rory out of the suit, which was whipped away, leaving him to pull on his more familiar jeans and hoody.

Outside, he and Jack stepped into a swirling snowstorm as bone-freezing wind beat against them. Rory caught his breath as pinpricks of snow hit him in the face. It hadn't been snowing when they had walked into the Bonville brothers' shop, and it was making up for lost time.

"I wish we were going home and ordering a takeaway," Jack said, hailing a taxi. As one pulled up and they climbed in, Rory couldn't have agreed more.

As the cab pushed its way through the slow-moving traffic towards Chelsea, Rory willed the tightening knot in the pit of his stomach to loosen.

The evening ahead of them had been planned to be a full De Lacy family gathering. Diana had been very put out, Jack had told him, when sudden work problems had prevented both his brother George and Caroline's husband, Tim, from coming to London; instead, they would be arriving the night before the wedding. Rory had given a silent cheer when Jack had told him the plan had fallen on its face. But Caroline would be there, this evening, and her irreverent chatter and good humour would be a godsend.

The taxi pulled up outside the tall and imposing Chelsea house. Rory had tried to like the house but couldn't. Its front was smooth and flat, and the sash windows always felt like eyes watching him. It was nothing like the Manor House, down in Polton Lacy, with its long gravel drive bordered with gnarly, mature trees.

I was so scared, the first time I went. Rory's lips curled up in a small smile. He'd come to love the house, with its soft grey stone, warm and mellow with age, and set amid the lush green Devonshire countryside. It was large and rambling, yet there was something welcoming and cosy about the place in the way the Chelsea house was not.

"Come on, let's get inside. I'm freezing my nuts off out here."

Jack gave Rory a nudge towards the half dozen steps leading up to the shiny black-painted door. By the time they set foot on the second step, it opened to reveal Diana, dressed in soft cashmere and a hint of Chanel No. 5.

"Come in, the pair of you." Diana ushered them in, and hugged them both in turn.

Rory peeked over her shoulder to see if Anne, the De Lacy housekeeper and cook, hovered in the background. Anne and her husband were part of the estate contingent who'd attend the wedding, but the woman who produced the best Devonshire cream tea to be found was nowhere to be seen.

Rory followed mother and son, chatting and laughing, up the steep and narrow staircase into a room that was decorated in the same style as the Morning Room at the Manor House.

Family photographs adorned pale yellow-and-white-striped walls, and a couple of classic squishy sofas loaded up with cushions gave the room an elegant yet at the same time homely feel. To one side of the roaring fire stood a tall, bushy Christmas tree decorated with red and green bows and traditional gingerbread men. Rory suppressed a smile. No cheap plastic tree for Diana, and definitely no alternative Christmas fairy, and as for harnessed and handlebar moustached gingerbread men...

"Umpf!"

Rory staggered back, literally knocked from his thoughts as two boys barrelled into him.

"Uncle Rory! Uncle Rory!" the boys shouted in unison as they attempted to climb up his body, using him as a human ladder.

"Monsters, dismount at once." Diana's crystal clear voice was enough for Hugo and Henry to run, screeching, from the room.

"Come here, you two." A second later Caroline was wrapping him and Jack in a warm and generous hug.

"Sherry?" Diana asked, a finely drawn eyebrow cocked, when Rory and Jack were huddled on the same sofa as Caroline.

"Another for me, please. It really is rather delish," Caroline said.

Diana's brow seemed to arch higher, into her hairline. Rory pulled out a paper tissue and pretended to blow his nose to cover his simmering laughter. Diana didn't need to say a word in order to convey exactly what she was thinking.

"It's Christmas and an extra special one at that. And it'll only go off if we don't drink it." Caroline beamed as she held out her glass.

"Good sherry does not *go off*. As you well know." Diana poured them all generous glasses.

Rory hummed his delight, and Jack smiled and winked at him.

Bone dry, nutty, and with the merest hint of salt,

the golden-hued alcohol melted every one of Rory's muscles. It was, as Caroline said, delish.

"Where's Dad?" Jack asked.

"He had some business to attend to, but he'll be in time for supper. He—"

The door flew open, accompanied by screams — and barks.

"Oh, my God!" Rory thrust his drink into Jack's hand and leaped up. Bounding towards him, all wagging tail and lolling tongue, was a chunky golden labrador.

Rory sank to his knees and pulled the dog into a hard cuddle.

"Badger," he said, over and over, burying his face into the labrador's soft fur, breathing in his warm, doggy scent.

The dog's name caught in his throat, and tears welled up in Rory's eyes. This wasn't any dog, this wasn't any family pet, this was *Badger*, his four-footed furry friend, his near-constant companion and ultimate saviour during that first visit to Jack's parents.

"We thought it would be a lovely surprise for you," Caroline said. "We know how much he means to you." She sniffed and blinked, wiping away a rogue tear.

"Thank you, thank you so much." Rory couldn't keep the smile off his face. "Did you know?" he said, looking at Jack.

"Mum may have mentioned a special guest was accompanying them to town."

Rory held Jack's gaze. He'd thank him for the surprise in his own special way later.

The Monsters dragged Badger off to a corner of the room, where boys and dog played happily, and more sherry was poured.

"The cake was delivered to the hotel earlier today," Diana said when they were all settled. "Naturally, I went to inspect that everything was as it should be. Rory, your friend is to be congratulated. It's quite the most beautiful wedding cake I've ever seen."

Rory smiled, catching Jack's eye in the briefest of glances. On the way over, they had wondered how long it would take before Diana started to talk about the wedding. He'd beaten Jack hands down.

"Jolly brave of you to make your own wedding cake," Caroline said.

"Rory's the best baker in London, so who else was good enough to do it?" Jack gave the back of Rory's neck a gentle squeeze.

Rory pushed into Jack's touch, the unspoken message of *just go with the flow* was as loud and clear as it was silent.

"Why did you get somebody else to ice it, though?"

"Because icing to that standard is an art in itself, and my friend Sally's the best around. She does a lot of work for magazines, TV, films, and so on." Rory took a sip of sherry. He had no doubts about his own skill, but when it came to icing, Sally was on another level.

"It's as well your friend is used to having her work photographed for the press as I've arranged for a photographer to take some shots of the cake tomorrow, for a piece in London Society magazine.'

Silence smothered the room.

"*What?*" Rory stared at Diana, snapping shut his jaw, which had dropped open. "Why—why would you do that? I didn't know about this. Did you, Jack?" Rory turned and searched Jack's face, but the thin, hard line of his fiancé's lips and the flinty glint in his eyes was all the answer Rory needed.

Rory turned back to Diana, his hands beginning to ache as they curled into tight fists in his lap.

"This is our day, mine and Jack's," he said, not dropping his gaze from Diana's. "We don't want it turned into a circus."

"It won't be—"

"We don't want any part of our wedding day turning up in a magazine, no matter how smart it is. There'll be an article to go with it, won't there?"

"For Christ's sake, Mum, were you even going to tell us about this?" Jack glared across at Diana. "We didn't agree this, and we don't want it. Whoever it is, cancel them first thing in the morning."

From the other sofa, Diana gazed at them, seemingly as calm and in control as always, but Rory wasn't fooled. Two small but bright red patches appeared on her cheeks. Boris, the suddenly returned cousin, and a handful of long-serving estate workers being added to the guest list was one thing. But *this?* She'd overstepped the mark, but backing down didn't come easy to her.

Thanks, Diana. We've been here before, remember?

The memory of an early morning conversation, just him and Diana, on his first visit to the Manor House… Jack exploding in anger, threatening to haul them both back to London, threatening to walk out on his family… Rory shivered.

"I'm sorry." She brushed a non-existent spec from her cashmere skirt. "The photographer is the daughter of an old friend, somebody I know through my charity work. There will be no article, no intrusion upon your privacy, just a photograph of an exquisite wedding cake along with the names of the grooms." She shrugged. "I'll call her and ask her to stand down. It'll be a little awkward, but then I shouldn't have put you in the situation I have. I apologise."

"London Society magazine? It's so smart you can only get it delivered on subscription, and it arrives in a plain wrapper. I'm sure the postman must wonder what I'm having delivered each month." Caroline sniggered. "Every time it pops through the letterbox, I give a little curtsy and experience an overwhelming urge to launch into the chorus of Land of Hope and Glory."

Caroline laughed, and the tightness in Rory's shoulders began, just a little, to thaw as he looked at her with a wan smile.

"Honestly, Rory," she said, leaning across and squeezing his knee. "I wouldn't worry. You won't have the paparazzi rushing to your door in a frenzy of wedding cake icing. London Society magazine is hardly Heat or OK!. I think it's safe to say it's got a somewhat narrow and limited readership."

"Perhaps I can get hold of Fiona now or leave a message at least. I'll just find my phone," Diana said as she stood.

"Just a photo, nothing else? No article?" Rory said.

Diana stopped in her tracks and cocked her head to one side as she thought. "Other than the grooms, just the name of the cake maker and the one who iced it. So, your names and your friend's. Nothing more. A short sentence or two at most."

Rory turned to Jack and locked eyes with him. *Are we, am I, making too much of this?*

Jack returned his silent question with a barely-there shrug.

Rory looked back at Diana. He wasn't concerned about any mention of The Bakehouse or him as the baker — God knows, they had more work on than they could handle, and he wasn't going to let his and Jack's business be part of their wedding day — but Sally had only just started up on her own…

He turned back to Jack, who gave him a sure nod of the head, and Rory smiled his reply. Jack knew exactly what he was thinking, and his nod was his agreement.

"As long as the focus is on the decoration and Sally's skill, we'll agree to it."

"I don't want you to agree to anything you're uncomfortable with," Diana said.

Perhaps you should have thought about that before… but Rory bit back on the words.

"As Ro said, we'll agree to it on the condition the spotlight's on Sally. But I hope there aren't any more surprises coming our way?" Jack levelled his gaze at his mother.

Diana inclined her head, not a hair out of place in her silvery classic bob. She looked as unruffled and calm as ever, with no hint of the flush that for a moment had stained her cheeks.

Sudden squeals and barking from the corner of the room had them all turning around. Hugo and Henry had taken some of the decorations from the Christmas tree and had decorated Badger.

"Good heavens, boys," Caroline exclaimed, abandoning her drink and leaping up to go to Badger's rescue.

Rory didn't think the good-natured dog who always seemed to have a smile on his face needed or wanted rescuing. And he certainly didn't seem to mind being the recipient of the boys' decorating skills. The Monsters had covered him in bows and tied a Christmas star to his wagging tail, draped gingerbread men over his ears, and from somewhere had found a Santa Claus hat which flopped over his head.

Jack started to laugh, rich and gravelly, smoothing out the awkwardness of the last few minutes. Rory released a long but quiet breath as tension began to drain from him.

"Hold on a minute, Caro," Jack said, fishing his phone from his pocket. "I've got to get a picture of this."

With photos taken, Caroline stripped the dog bare of his Christmas finery amid Badger's barks and howls of protest from the boys.

More drinks were poured, and talk turned to Polton Lacy. Rory sat back, letting it wash over him.

The door swung open, and Rory smiled up at the man who strode into the room. Sir Roger De Lacy, his soon-to-be father-in-law.

"Dad." Jack bounded up, and father and son gave

each other a long, hard hug; the hug Rory received was no less welcoming.

"Good to see you both. Stay the night if you want. The weather's filthy, the snow's coming down heavier than ever." Roger brushed his hand across his hair, dislodging melting snowflakes. "Sorry I wasn't here to greet you both but I had business in the City, with my broker. Ah, thank you Diana," he said, accepting a drink from his wife with a warm, wide smile. "When's supper? I'm absolutely ravenous."

CHAPTER SIXTEEN

"Rory's very quiet this evening." Roger said in an undertone.

"He's tired. The business is demanding, which is good, but with the wedding..." Jack let his words trail off.

There had been no more prenuptial surprises. No announcements that Country Life, Hare & Hounds, The Lady magazine, or any number of the up-market periodicals his mother subscribed to wanted to run a feature on his and Rory's wedding. There was no alteration to the menu, no further additions to the guest list, or a thousand and one sudden changes. Nothing further to muddy the waters, send ripples across the pond, or throw Rory into a stress-filled panic.

Roger huffed. "Marriage is a big step, Jack. It's not something to be taken lightly. If neither of you was overawed by the commitment you're about to give to each other, then *I* would be more than a little worried."

Jack stared at his father. "We don't take it lightly. Why do you think we would? It's what we both want more than anything else, but it's not going to make a huge amount of difference to our day-to-day lives."

"On a daily basis, most likely not, but you will *feel* differently about your life together, and about each other. I guarantee it."

Caroline, on the other side of Roger, said something, snatching Roger's attention away. Jack took a sip of his wine, rolling it around over his tongue as he considered his father's words.

He didn't want to feel differently about Rory. How could the way he felt now get any better? Their lives would change because that's what life did, and it would do that whether they were married or not.

Sudden squeals of laughter broke through his thoughts. Jack looked across to Hugo and Henry, the pair of them rolling around in the corner of the room with the ever good-tempered Badger. The Monsters weren't badly behaved — or not much. He preferred to think of his nephews as lively and irrepressible, and he loved them to bits. He smiled, as he watched them play.

He settled back in his chair and shifted his gaze to his mother and Rory.

The earlier tension had disappeared. The arrival of his father, just his presence a calming influence, and Caroline's upbeat, irreverent chatter throughout dinner had also played its part in smoothing down any remaining jagged edges. Jack had caught his sister's eye earlier, and the small, narrow-eyed smile she'd given him had been enough to confirm his suspicions that she was working hard to make the atmosphere bright and breezy and to keep it there. And it had worked, if the nodding heads and relaxed body language both Rory and his mother were displaying, on the other side of the large, round table was anything to go by.

And thank fuck for that.

After dinner, they made their way back to the lounge, collapsing once more into squashy sofas and comfy armchairs. Jack threw his arm around Rory's shoulders, and a bubble of warmth burst deep in his chest as Rory leant into him.

"Yummy," said Caroline, and she took a sip of the brandy Roger handed her. "You've brought out the big guns tonight."

Roger laughed. "It's not every day my youngest son gets married," he said, throwing a smile Jack and Rory's way.

The main light had been switched off, and the room was lit by both free-standing and table lamps. With the warm orange glow from the fire, the room was snug, and for the first time that evening, Jack was truly feeling mellow.

"At what time will you be coming here the day before? You'll be in time for supper, I take it?"

"What do you mean?" Jack looked at his mother. He had no idea what she was talking about.

"You'll be here the night before the wedding. Both of you."

"It's the first I've heard about it." This wasn't a detail he would have forgotten about. He turned to Rory, who was looking at him in confusion and consternation.

"It's the sensible arrangement. What were you expecting to do?"

Something else sprung on them, something else not agreed beforehand.

"That we would come over on Christmas Eve. The ceremony's not until 3:00 pm."

Diana's brow wrinkled as though, Jack thought, she was having difficulty understanding his argument.

"Jack, why would you want to battle your way across London, on your wedding day and in this weather?"

The irritation in Diana's voice ratcheted up a

notch, and Jack ground his teeth. *For God's sake, wasn't the awkward moment earlier enough?*

"It's four stops on the Underground, Mum. Hardly what I'd call *battling*."

Diana huffed. "But everything you need is here. It's far better we're all in one place, and with this dreadful weather... Surely you can see the sense?"

Implacable blue eyes met implacable blue eyes. Jack chose his words with care.

"I know what you say makes a lot of sense—no, hear me out," Jack said when he saw she was about to interrupt. "But we're closing the shop early the day before, and we're going to have a quiet evening at home together. It's what we both want. I'm sorry if I've upset your plans, Mum, but it's how we want to spend our last evening together before we get married."

They would shut the door, the two of them alone, just him and Rory, before the world went crazy.

Diana threw her hands into the air. It was a rare show of exasperation and irritation.

"We've already talked about this."

"Have we? I certainly don't remember."

"Rory, what do you think?" Diana turned her piercing blue eyes to Rory.

Oh no. No, no, no.

The conversation, if what felt like a battle of wills

could be called that, had been between him and his mother, and that's where it was going to stay.

"Mum—"

Rory squeezed his thigh, and Jack looked down into Rory's deep brown eyes. *Let me*, they were saying.

"We're not getting married until three o'clock. We can get here early in the day. Perhaps we could all have breakfast together?"

It was the balm Jack needed. A simple suggestion had averted the disaster of him and his mother staring at each other, neither giving in, as they glowered over a chasm of conflicting wants and desires. Not that his mother ever glowered, but still.

"I think that's a very workable and may I say a very sensible compromise. Rory, thank you. Diana, it will work perfectly well," Roger said.

Jack narrowed his eyes at his father, relaxed and nursing his brandy. He wasn't fooled by his level and reasonable tone. Behind the calm words was the unmistakable message his dad was sending to his mum: *this* is what is going to happen, no further argument.

"Yes, come for breakfast," Diana said after a moment's hesitation. "I just assumed..." She flicked non-existent dust from the lap of her cashmere skirt.

That's your problem, Mum, you just assume...

Jack glanced down at Rory and pulled him in a little closer. They'd piloted their way through the evening's choppy waters, and now all Jack wanted was to get him and Rory home as soon as possible.

"We have to go as we've another early start in the morning." He gave Rory's shoulder a gentle squeeze, a silent signal that he was not to contradict the lie. Mabel was opening up for them in the morning.

Amid goodbyes and arrangements for their arrival on Christmas Eve, Rory and Jack stepped out onto the snow-bound street.

"Jesus," Jack breathed.

"I don't remember anything about staying the night before."

"No." Jack linked his arm with Rory's. With heads down against the fast-falling snow, they began to pick their way towards the Tube station. "It was just my mother assuming, the way she's assumed throughout the wedding preparations." He turned to Rory, putting his arm out to stop him. "I'm sorry."

"What for?"

But Rory was looking at him with a small *I told you so* smile on his face, and he had every right to do it.

"For letting her have too much of a free hand over the last few months. Knowing how she would be should have—"

The weight of Rory's gloved fingers pressed against his lips, stopping his stumbling apology.

"Come on, let's get home. We can have a snowball. Or three."

Jack laughed and took Rory's hand, leading them towards the one place he wanted to be.

Home.

CHAPTER SEVENTEEN

"Jack, what are you doing?" Rory laughed as he made a half-hearted attempt to pull Jack's hands from his eyes as he was guided to the kitchen.

"I told you, it's a surprise." Jack's laughter rippled through his own words. "It's our special night. You know? The one before our wedding? The night alone we fought so valiantly for as we faced down the dragon."

"Jack! Don't be mean about your mum," Rory spluttered. Yes, they'd faced down a determined Diana, but it *was* mean for Jack to call her a dragon. Or kind of.

"Da-*dar!*" Jack pulled his hands away.

Rory blinked hard. The little kitchen table was set with crisp, white linen, plain china, and wine glasses, with the centre decorated with flowers. Candles were dotted all around, casting a flickering background glow — which also managed to cast a glow on the devastation scattered on the countertop and in the sink. But none of that mattered; all that did was the perfect little table set for two in their own private restaurant.

"I could have set up in the living room, but then you'd have known, and it would have spoilt the surprise." Jack's lips lifted in a sheepish smile.

"It's perfect."

Rory coiled his arms around Jack's neck and brushed a soft kiss to his lips, savouring their warmth. Jack sighed and slipped his arms around Rory's waist as Rory nuzzled into his fiancé's neck.

"Thank you," Rory murmured. "Thank you so much. Not just for tonight, but for everything you've done for me. If it wasn't for you…"

Rory looked up as Jack eased him out of his arms and gazed down at him.

"That's in the past. What's important is that we found each other. That's what matters."

Rory nodded, the words in his throat too hard and heavy to speak.

Jack was right, of course he was. They had travelled so far since their fateful meeting, forging a life together that had taken them to the cusp of marriage. But Jack was right. Tonight was about enjoying who they were and what they would become.

Rory grinned in delight when Jack seated him, with a flourish of a tea towel, at the little table. His grin turned to laughter when Jack produced plate after plate, meze-style.

It was a strange assortment. No one plate of food went with another, but each was heaped high with the picnic-style food they loved. Curried pieces of this, marinated that; creamy dips and fluffy breads. Cocktail sausages and mini sausage rolls. And mince pies. All of it washed down with champagne chilled to perfection.

"The Bakehouse?" Rory held up a perfect package of loveliness. Of course they were. He'd recognise his handiwork anywhere, but how he was going to manage one after the feast Jack had produced…

"Where else would they be from? These are selling like hotcakes, or should I say hot pies," Jack said with a mischievous grin. "I almost had to smuggle these out, they were going so fast. I thought we deserved some. We haven't eaten nearly enough mince pies this Christmas."

Rory laughed. "Really? Every time I bake a batch, half of them go missing straight away—into your mouth."

"I can neither confirm nor deny. But such perfect little morsels deserve to be eaten warm."

"I don't think I could eat another thing." Rory slumped back into his seat. He was full and sated and, for what felt like the first time in ages, truly relaxed. He looked at the plate. "Perhaps I could manage one, with a glass of dessert wine." It would be such a shame to fall at the last hurdle when Jack had made so much effort...

"Anything you want, Kincaid."

They met each other's eyes across the table, holding their gaze.

"It's the last time I'll call you that," Jack said, his voice low and quiet.

Rory nodded. In a few hours, Rory Kincaid would step back as Rory De Lacy stepped forward.

Jack pushed himself up from the table and laid a kiss on top of Rory's head.

"You go through; I'll get it sorted."

In the living room, Rory snuggled into the sofa. Relaxation melted his muscles and bones, and he snuggled down further. This was what they'd stood up to Diana for, for this, just the two of them. He didn't want the fuss, all the family, or to sleep in a house that always felt as if it were looking at him with some kind of silent disapproval. Him and Jack together, tonight and always, in their comfortable, comforting, untidy home. *This* was what he wanted. He closed his eyes.

"Hey, you. No falling asleep on me."

Rory blinked up at Jack. Asleep? Had he been? Maybe for a second or two...

Jack put the tray on the coffee table and sat down, and together they bit into the warm fruit-filled little pies.

Rich and crumbly pastry melted in his mouth; sweet and buttery, it was a contrast to the sharp vine fruits that packed out the centre. Pride warmed Rory's heart. The recipe was his own, traditional but with a modern twist, just like much of what they sold in The Bakehouse.

"At the risk of sounding big-headed, I'm going to say these are really good." Rory sucked the sweet juice from his fingertips.

"It's not big-headed, it's the truth."

"I never thought it would go so well, the business I mean. The Bakehouse has gone beyond everything I'd hoped for." Rory bent forward and stared intently at the heaped-up little pies.

Was this the time to say something? When so much was happening, wasn't it just another thing to be added to their already teetering load? But with the two of them, in the comforting warmth and loose and relaxed, the pressing need to give voice to his thoughts was too much to resist — because he knew Jack shared them.

"I was in that little café a few days ago, the one in Soho we've been to before."

"Barista Boys, you mean? The one in the narrow side street?"

Rory nodded. "The trade they were doing, it was phenomenal. I thought we were doing well until I saw what was happening there. And it got me thinking. About The Bakehouse and our future, and where we go from here. I know you've been thinking, too." Rory turned to Jack, brown eyes locking with blue.

"Ro, it's perfect." Jack's voice was low, quiet, but the tremble of excitement was unmistakable. "I've been wanting to talk to you for ages, about expanding. Not just making the bakery bigger but making it *more*, but with the wedding—"

"And my constant fretting over it?" Rory arched his brows, and Jack responded with a sheepish smile. How could he blame Jack for keeping his thoughts to himself, even if he'd already guessed what they were, when *he* had been freaking out every two minutes...?

"No. God, no. It's not that at all." A small frown puckered Jack's brow, and he bit down on his lower lip as his gaze shifted to the fire.

His thinking face... Rory waited for Jack to continue.

"I suppose," Jack said slowly, carefully, "that I didn't want you to think I was trying to make us run before we could walk. But I couldn't see the harm in talking to the commercial estate agent who's handling the shop next door." Jack turned to him, and Rory couldn't help but smile. He'd have been blind to miss the spark of excitement in Jack's eyes. "He said the freeholder's keen to sell up, so a deal should be possible. But the agent also thinks permission to knock through *and* be granted a license to convert to a bakery-café won't be a problem. Ours is the sort of business the local council wants to see more of. We can do this, Ro. I know we can."

Rory's jaw dropped. Where he'd been pondering, Jack had already taken action. Could they do it? Jack believed they could... Trepidation bubbled up inside him, but so did excitement.

"But that's not all," Jack said, squeezing his hands tighter.

Not all? There was *more?*

"We should think about opening other branches. A small, up-market chain of Bakehouses. No more than half a dozen, all in key locations. Do you think I'm mad or drunk? It's got to be one or the other."

"There's brandy in the mince pies, but... You really mean this, don't you?"

"Yes, I do. I believe in it because I believe in us."

The thought was exciting and terrifying. But hadn't it been like that in the very beginning, when Jack had first raised the idea of them going into business together to open a small bakery?

"I haven't thought that far ahead. I was only looking at adding a small café area, but..." Rory's thoughts waged war. What Jack was proposing... Yes, no, maybe. *Yes.* Yes, of course they could do it.

Couldn't they?

He took a deep breath to try to settle his racing heart. "Do you really think we can do it?" Rory snuggled into Jack.

"I think we can do anything if we put our minds to it," Jack said as he pulled Rory in close.

They cuddled in silence for a minute, or ten, or thirty, Rory didn't know how long as he lay against Jack, feeling the regular in-out of his breath, and the sweep of his fingers through his hair. *So much to think about...*

"Sometimes you have to take a leap of faith and run headlong into the future."

"About expanding? Yes, I suppose so."

Rory shivered, as Jack swept his fingers through his hair, the tingle delicious as it danced along the length of his spine.

"About life," Jack said quietly.

Rory frowned. Just two words. Yet there was a weightiness about them, as though they were more than the sum of their parts.

"Jack?" Rory shifted, and gazed up at his fiancé. "What—?"

"Come on. We've got a big day in front of us tomorrow." Jack leaped up and pulled Rory to his feet, and into his arms.

Their lips met in a bruising kiss. As tongues found tongues, whatever questions Rory had, they melted away as *tomorrow* and everything it would bring pulled him in and held him tight.

CHAPTER EIGHTEEN

"I can't get this bloody thing done up." Jack unknotted his tie and tried again for what felt like the fiftieth time, and each time he tried, his hands only shook worse than before.

His father batted his hands away and tied the silk tie in a perfect Eton knot.

"There. Now leave it alone and put your jacket on."

Jack shrugged on the slate grey, fine-wool jacket, the deep cerise silk lining exhaling a soft, sibilant sigh as it slid against the palest pink silk of his shirt. The suit was a slim cut, classic in its simplicity. He and Rory had rejected the suggestion of morning suits — too fussy, they'd argued — and as the suit wrapped itself around him like a second skin, he knew he and Rory had made the right decision.

Rory. Jack's stomach clenched in excited, nervy anticipation. On another floor of the Chelsea house, Rory was with Caroline. He smiled; the look of relief that had broken out over Rory's face earlier, at breakfast, when Caroline had quietly asked if he wanted help in getting ready had been almost comical. His sister wasn't just his husband-to-be's future sister-in-law, she was Rory's good friend.

Are his hands shaking? Will Caroline have to tie the knot in his tie?

"You look perfect, Jack."

"What?" Jack looked up, meeting his mother's blue eyes. Wrapped up in his thoughts, he'd not noticed her come into the bedroom.

"But the finishing touch is the buttonhole."

Diana stepped forward, and attached the cream rose bud, its petals on the cusp of opening. She stepped back, and looked between her son and husband as she dabbed at her eyes with a paper tissue.

"Mum?" She was crying. He took a step forward. "Mum?" he croaked.

"We're so proud of you, Jack. You're the best of sons, and the best of men. And as for the man you're going to be marrying today, we are *so, so* glad it's Rory who's going to become a De Lacy."

Jack leant down and placed a kiss on his mother's cheek. "Thank you. For everything," he whispered. He blinked at his parents through wavy, misted vision. "Do you think I'll do him proud today?" He gave a shaky laugh as he opened his arms.

"You will, Jack," Roger said, nodding. "The way you'll do us all, and yourself, proud."

A small tap on the door, and Anne's voice, telling them the Daimler was waiting downstairs.

Jack drew in a shuddering breath and squared his shoulders.

"Best be off, I suppose. I've a wedding to go to."

"I think this might be called for."

Caroline tore the foil from the neck of the champagne bottle and, in an effortless twist, released the cage and cork. A fine smoke drifted upwards as she poured two glasses.

"Just a sip. My stomach's doing somersaults as it is."

"Then this will put it right. Pol Roger, better than antacid any day of the week. Go on, it'll calm you down. My chief bridesmaid and I guzzled a whole bottle between us just an hour before I was due to walk up the aisle. Soothed my nerves no end. Cheers."

They chinked glasses, and Rory took the sip he didn't want until he tasted it.

"Oh."

"Not such a bad idea after all?" Caroline smiled.

No, it wasn't a bad idea at all.

Breakfast had been a loud and lively affair, with all the immediate De Lacy family crowded around the table in the basement kitchen. The chat had been non-stop, as had the squeals from Hugo and Henry, and Badger's gruff bark. He and Jack had grabbed a few minutes alone, in the snow-drenched garden, before each had been whisked away. Rory sipped on his champagne. The next time he and Jack would be together, it would be to stand before the registrar.

"Top up?"

"Hmm? Oh, erm, just a little." The churn in his stomach really had stopped. "Thank you." Rory hesitated, licking his lips before he spoke again. "Not for this, but for, well, you know."

Caroline looked at him with a raised brow, a crooked smile lifting her lips. Rory grinned. She and Jack were so alike.

"You couldn't get a better man than Jack, you know, but then neither could he."

"Do you really think so? Your parents must have—"

"My parents only wanted what was best for Jack, and they found the best in you. Don't have any doubts about that, ever."

Caroline looked at her watch. "Time to put on that

gorgeous suit of yours. I'll leave you to do that, as I really shouldn't be seeing my future brother-in-law in his underpants. I'll be back in a few minutes to give you the once-over."

Caroline disappeared, and Rory stared at the suit and shirt hanging up and waiting for him. Fine, slate grey wool, the shirt the palest of pink, and a deep magenta silk tie, the same as Jack's, down to the last detail. He ran his fingers across the soft wool; never in his wildest dreams had he ever thought he'd wear something so fine. He smiled. All those fittings with the creepy little Bonville brothers had been worth it after all.

Trousers and shirt, socks, and shoes so polished he could almost see his face in them. His jacket would go on just before he and Caroline left. He slipped on the watch Jack had presented to him in the shop near to the Leadenhall. It was Jack's gift to him, and when he'd said he had nothing for Jack, his words had been stopped with a press of fingers to lips and the words 'you're my gift'.

A brief knock on the door and Caroline came back in.

"Let me help you with the tie. I'm something of an expert with Eton knots."

Caroline frowned in concentration as deft fingers did their work before she helped him on with the jacket and pinned the cream rose bud to his buttonhole.

"Oh, you look amazing. Here, see."

She gave him a gentle push towards the freestanding mirror in the corner of the room.

"Oh."

Rory hardly recognised the man who stared back at him. The boy who'd huddled on a doorstep in the depth of a London winter two years before was nowhere to be seen in the elegant man reflected in the mirror. Rory's throat closed up; he blinked and swept the heel of his hand across his eyes. That boy may have gone, but he would never, ever be forgotten.

The buzz of his phone, on the table beneath the window, pulled him back to the present.

Who—? He plucked it up, his eyes widening in surprise when he saw the caller display.

He met Caroline's curious gaze.

"Sonia," he croaked. "My mother."

Caroline mouthed a silent *oh* before she slipped from the room.

Rory tapped to accept the call, pushing the phone tight to his ear.

"Rory? Rory, are you there?" Sonia's voice, so clear she could have been in the room with him; he glanced around, expecting almost to see her.

"Yes. You're, erm, in Spain?"

"I am. But I, I didn't want, couldn't…" she said, her words stumbling.

Rory heard her pull in a deep breath.

"I kept thinking about you, getting married today. I couldn't let today go past and not call. Then I realised I didn't know what time, or—"

"Thank you. For calling. I'm glad you did."

"Are you? Really?" Her voice was quiet, unsure.

Rory nodded as he spoke. "I am. It makes me…" He closed his eyes. *No longer feel quite so much like an orphan.* He bit back the words. Hard words, cruel even, and today there was no place for hardness and cruelty. "I'm glad you rang, that we're talking today. It means a lot."

"Thank you. Thank you for—well, just thank you."

The discreet tap and the door opening caught his attention. Caroline's head appeared around the jamb. He smiled as he held up his hand.

"Perhaps you could email some photos across? When you get the time?"

"Of course I will. Lots of them. I've got to go now. Can't have him thinking I've stood him up."

Sonia laughed. "Good luck, Rory, but I reckon you've already got luck and a whole lot more on your side."

"Okay?" Caroline asked as she advanced into the room.

Rory threw his phone onto the bed and nodded.

"I'm glad she called. It makes me feel…"

"Not quite so alone in the world?"

Rory shrugged, and sniffed. "Yeah. Stupid, isn't it? Because alone is the one thing I'm not."

Caroline answered with a soft, gentle smile.

"No, you're not. Time to go, Rory." Caroline laid a hand on his shoulder. "Come, Jack's waiting for you."

CHAPTER NINETEEN

"He's late." Jack looked at his watch for the tenth, for the hundredth, for the thousandth time. He paced the small anteroom from the plain Adams fireplace with its bed of smouldering logs, to the tall sash window, and back again.

"Stop panicking, Jack. There's plenty of time. Caroline's with him, don't forget. If they've got caught up in traffic, she'd have rung by now." Roger's words, as calm and unperturbed as ever.

Jack glanced out of the window. The snow had been falling steadily for the last couple of days but had come down heavily overnight and continued to fall, making a near-solid white blanket.

What if they've got stuck? What if the car's skidded? What if it's rolling, speeding out of control on the treacherous roads? What if—?

Jack gasped as the Daimler, as long and sleek as the one he'd arrived in, pulled into the hotel's small courtyard, coming to a smooth stop at the entrance. Doors opened, and Caroline stepped out first, protected by the canopy which stretched between the door and the kerbside. A moment later, Rory followed her, and Jack's heart clenched so hard his breath burned in his chest.

He looks— Jack dragged at his eyes, smearing away the tears that threatened to brim over.

"You see? No need to have got yourself into such a pickle."

Jack turned to his dad and smiled. "You were always saying that to me when I was a kid."

Roger huffed. "You haven't changed much since then, Jack. And I'm very happy for it."

They both turned at the voices just the other side of the door.

"I think it's time I took my place next to your mother." With a quick squeeze of Jack's shoulder, Roger disappeared through the far door, leading to the Garden Room where the ceremony was to take place, leaving Jack alone for a moment.

The door opened on silent hinges and Jack sucked in his breath as Rory paused on the threshold. They stared at each other, neither moving for a moment before Rory stepped through and closed the door behind him with a soft click. Jack swallowed. Rory's dark, heavy hair was stark against his pale skin. His eyes seemed bigger, their rich chocolate brown deeper than he'd ever seen them. Jack swallowed again. Rory was stunning, beautiful, and his.

"You look..." Jack shook his head, lost for words.

"You don't scrub up so badly yourself."

Jack laughed, Rory's lighthearted comment pinpricking the charged atmosphere that filled the small room.

"Worth all those fittings with the creepy Bonville brothers?" Jack smiled, but it faded from his lips with his next words. "You're sure about today? No last minute..." He swallowed as his words died on his tongue.

"Never. Never, ever think it." Rory stepped forward, closing the gap between them. "Never," he murmured as he placed the lightest of kisses to Jack's lips.

Jack released a trembling sigh.

Never, ever think it.

The light tap on the door leading to the Garden Room was the signal it was time. As it opened, they clasped their hands together, firm, warm, and strong, and walked forward.

❄

Rory gasped and turned to Jack, who answered with an *I told you so* smile.

Two huge Christmas trees stood sentinel on either side of the tall window where the registrar stood waiting for them. Each was a mirror image of the other, adorned with bows and pinecones and topped with a simple star. Two large fireplaces, on either side of the room, their mantles tumbling with holly and ivy, crackled with flaming logs, releasing their soft resinous scent.

The crystal chandelier hanging from the centre of the ceiling flickered with mellow candlelight, making the light warm and soft. Outside, daylight was fading into dark over the winter wonderland that was the garden, its trees and bushes heavy with still-falling snow.

"It's beautiful, Jack, so beautiful," Rory whispered, turning to Jack and smiling.

The applause was a thunderclap, shattering through the Garden Room. Everybody rose as one as they were greeted by cheers and whistles, joyous laughter, and smiles.

Rory swung his head from side to side. Jack's family at the front; faces from Polton Lacy; his and Jack's London friends; the flash of a copper-coloured beehive and a cherry-red dress, Mabel waving, her mouth stretched wide in a scarlet-lipped grin, and next to her with a shy smile, Lance.

They approached the registrar, and quiet fell upon the room, as sudden as it had exploded into loud, joy-filled pandemonium.

"Rory, Jack? Are you ready?" the round-faced, motherly registrar asked.

"Yes," Rory and Jack croaked together.

"Then we shall begin..."

The world contracted. Everything around Rory faded until there was nobody other than him and Jack and the soft, measured voice of the registrar, intoning the age-old words Rory had never, ever believed would be words said for *him*.

"If anybody knows of any lawful impediment..."

Rory sucked in a huge breath. No, of course there wasn't, but...A deathly hush filled the Garden Room. Rory met Jack's eyes, and smiled. The registrar's voice, warm and smooth, was a low murmur to the loud beat of his heart.

"...do solemnly declare that I know not of any..."

Jack spoke the words loud and clear, each filling the warm room, his gaze levelled on Rory, steady and unwavering.

Rory repeated the same declaration, stumbling a little, clearing his throat before starting again. A gentle ripple of laughter swept through the room. Rory glanced at the gathering, and gave a shy, apologetic smile.

"Jack, Rory, I invite you to speak your vows."

Rory's heart stuttered as Jack clasped his hands, as warm, strong and sure as ever. A moment of silence, as Jack smiled into his eyes; his heart rate slowed and calmed. They'd agreed on a handful of simple words, because what more was there to say than—

"I love you, Rory. I always will. Now and for always, and more than you could ever know."

"Is that all?" The registrar raised her brows.

"It's enough," Jack answered, and she smiled her agreement.

"And Rory?" she asked.

"I love you, Jack. I always will. Now and for always, and more than you could ever know." Rory blinked hard, his eyes prickling with joyous tears.

"Will you exchange rings?"

Their rings, platinum bands engraved with their names and wedding date. Roger would present them for him and Jack to exchange, but Roger was seated with Diana, smiling and making no move to stand.

"Jack?"

"Look." Jack nodded back towards the door they had come through.

Rory followed his gaze. Badger sat before the closed door, his tongue lolling in his smiley face. *What*

—? And then he saw. Dangling from his collar was a small, black box.

"Badger, come," Jack called. The dog trotted towards them, the box swinging backwards and forwards, before he plonked himself down at Rory's feet and looked up at him, tail wagging from side to side.

"Oh, Jack." Rory pressed his hands to his mouth. Tears rolled down his cheeks. "I—I..."

"He's very special. We couldn't get married without him."

"No, I—*oh, Badger.*"

Rory bent down and swept the dog into his arms. "Badger," he said, over and over again, barely aware of the cheers and laughter erupting around him and the flash of cameras.

"Thank you, Jack. Thank you so much. This is the best wedding present I could ever have." Rory stood up, wiping at his tear-stained face. Badger barked his agreement, and the guests broke into renewed laughter.

Roger did stand this time. He came forward and detached the box from Badger's collar. "Side, Badger," he said, and the dog trotted away. Roger opened the box, and Jack took one of the presented rings, holding it out.

"I give you this ring as a sign of our marriage, and I call upon these persons here present to witness that I,

Jack Marcus Charles De Lacy, do take thee Rory Matthew Kincaid to be my lawfully wedded husband..."

Rory shook as Jack slipped the cool metal onto his finger. It was a perfect fit; he would never, ever take it off. It would be where it now was until his dying day.

With a trembling voice, Rory repeated the declaration, his eyes misting over as he slipped the band onto Jack's ring finger. He let out the long breath he'd been barely aware of holding as he smiled into Jack's clear blue eyes.

"Jack and Rory, you have both made the declarations prescribed by law and have made a solemn and binding contract in the presence of your witnesses here today. It therefore gives me great pleasure to declare that you are now legally married."

Cheers, laughter, more clapping of hands, the elegant room was again a riot of joy and happiness.

"Come here, De Lacy."

Rory was pulled into Jack's arms, his lips crushed with a hot, searing kiss. The whoops and cheers grew louder, and more cameras flashed.

"Jack," he said, breathless, when Jack released him. His face was hot, and he looked out over the gathered guests, feeling the flush burn in his cheeks.

Jack laughed. "I could kiss you forever, and I don't care who sees."

A small cough brought their attention back to the registrar. "The register..."

Some minutes later, in another elegant room decked out with Christmas trees and warmed by traditional log fires, Rory and Jack stood surrounded by friends and family.

"I am so proud of you both," Diana said, raising her champagne flute.

"Thank you, Diana, thank you. All of this," Rory said, looking about him, "it's beautiful, wonderful. It's so much more than I ever imagined. I..." He hesitated, the words heavy on his tongue. "I'm sorry if I, if I seemed ungrateful or was—"

Diana raised her hand.

"No. You weren't. Don't think that. You had enough to deal with, and I was honoured to be of assistance." She put her glass down and enveloped him in a tight, close hug and a soft cloud of Chanel No. 5.

"You're a De Lacy now, Rory," she whispered into his ear, "and Roger and I couldn't be happier." She released him and dabbed her eyes with a paper tissue.

"It is beautiful, Mum, it truly is. Thank you. For everything. Thank you so, so much." Jack wrapped Diana up in his arms for a long, loving hug.

A warm, rich, honied voice rose up around them. A bluesy, jazzy song sung with heart accompanied by a sonorous saxophone drifted like smoke up into the air.

"Oh my God." Rory slapped his hands to his mouth for the second time that afternoon.

Mabel stood between two huge flower arrangements, hips swaying, eyes closed as she sang into the microphone. Behind her, Lance was a virtuoso on the sax.

"What a wonderful surprise. I knew she sang but… and Lance, I didn't know he played." Rory gazed in wonder, between Mabel and Lance, and Jack.

"I heard her singing in the shop when you were out, and knew at once she had to sing for us, but I didn't know about Lance. He's a dark horse, that kid."

Amidst laughter and chatter and a change in tempo to an upbeat Motown number, Rory and Jack received hugs and kisses, slaps on backs, and more hugs and kisses as they were congratulated and congratulated again, and their glasses topped up.

"Ladies and gentlemen, if you would care to take your places…"

"Come on, I think we might have seats on the top table," Jack said with a wink, and Rory laughed as he let his husband lead him through.

CHAPTER TWENTY

"Hmmm, this is nice. Just the two of us."

Jack tightened his arms around Rory and dropped a kiss on top of his husband's head.

His husband. He'd never, ever get tired of saying those words.

Behind them, in the hotel, they'd left the revellers behind. He and Rory had caught each other's eye and smiled in silent agreement as they'd disengaged themselves from friends and family, donned their heavy coats, and some Wellington boots the hotel had miraculously produced, and made their way into the moonlit garden.

A burst of laughter and a cheer erupted in the hotel to chants of *Roger! Roger!* Jack grinned. When they'd made their escape, his dad had been attempting to do the twist with Mabel. The brief burst of hilarity settled into a background hum.

"It's been perfect, Jack, so much more than I ever imagined." Rory snuggled his back tighter against Jack, and sighed.

"That's because the two best people were there. Come on, let's take a walk."

Hand in hand, they made their way down the long garden, picking their way through the deep snow. It had finally stopped, but snow-burdened clouds scudded across the sky, blotting out, then revealing a bright full moon. Trees and shrubs, benches and statues, encased in snow, formed strange and eerie shapes. In the midst of the city, nothing stirred, and out of earshot of the revelries, all was silent.

Jack looked at his watch, so much like the one he'd presented to Rory in the little Leadenhall watchmaker's. Five minutes to midnight, when Christmas Eve would melt into Christmas Day.

"Happy?" Jack asked, but he didn't need Rory's answer in words. His answer was in his husband's smile, in the brightness of his eyes, and in the soft kiss Rory brushed across his lips.

"More than you could know."

They sank into each other's arms, holding tight to each other under the shadowy moonlight in the silent garden, a perfect moment of stillness and calm.

Light snow drifted down, feathery flakes turning thicker and fatter, the whiteness coming down heavier and settling hard on their heads and shoulders.

"Maybe we should go back inside," Rory said as he looked up into the sky.

"Not quite yet. Anyway, I couldn't do this if we went back in." Jack leant down and licked away a pillowy flake that had landed on the tip of Rory's nose.

Out of the night sky, the bells began to peal, slicing through the silence. First one church, then another, then more. The whole sky filled with the sound of bells, as they rang in Christmas Day.

"Jack, it's—"

"I know, darling. I know." Jack cupped his hands to Rory's face, drinking in every inch of his husband's face, committing every tiny part of this moment to memory, where it would forever be buried deep in his heart.

"I love you, Rory De Lacy."

Simple, unadorned words which said everything that needed to be said.

As the bells rang in a snowy Christmas morning, Jack and Rory De Lacy melted into a slow, soft kiss.

I love you, Rory. I love you so, so much...

EPILOGUE

Six Months Later

Rory's eyes widened. He looked out over The Bakehouse as he clutched a large tray of freshly baked cupcakes. Christmas pudding buttercream had been replaced by strawberry, rhubarb, and raspberry, the lighter flavours and the fruits of summer.

"Have you had your break yet?"

Rory eyed the queue snaking out the propped-open door, his gaze shifting to the dozen small, round tables they could never have accommodated if they hadn't secured the freehold on the shop next door and knocked through. Every single one of them was taken. Affluent parents with babies and small children, students tapping into laptops, couples and singles scrolling through mobile phones. Every one of them drinking barista-style coffees, and tucking into cakes and sandwiches.

Mabel shrugged. "Not yet but that's okay. I'll wait until it's calmed down a bit. We haven't stopped all day," Mabel said, between handing over bagged-up muffins to a young woman with a small child, and plucking a ciabatta loaf from the shelf behind her. "It's been pandemonium. Good job we've got the new guys on board because Lance and I couldn't have coped. Yes, sweetie, what can I get you...?"

Rory glanced across at Cade and Ritchie and smiled. With his rainbow Mohican and safety pin piercing in one eyebrow, Mabel's cousin, working the shiny chrome coffee maker with effortless ease, was a living, breathing version of Bunty, the punk rocker Christmas fairy.

The odd couple, Jack had named the pair, and it was easy to see why. Ritchie, with his white-blond hair, crisp and conservative, and his just as crisp and conservative white shirt, the odd couple was exactly what they were. But when they looked at each other, their eyes lighting up and their faces dissolving into soppy, mushy grins... Rory smiled. He knew all about eyes lighting up and daft smiles...

The door flew open, and Jack strode in. His husband. Rory shivered. Those two words, just six months old, still had the power to send a tingle down his spine. Jack threw a wink at him as he took his place behind the counter.

"Deliveries all done. I'll take over now, Mabel."

"This is good." Jack stretched out on the sofa, warm air from the slung-open windows a soft breath on his skin. It had been a long, packed day, just like every day. Rory snuggled into him.

"It sure is. I love how busy The Bakehouse is, but it just makes me appreciate getting home and closing the door on it all the more. You know, I don't think our life could be better."

Jack swept his fingers through Rory's hair. Yes, their life was good. The Bakehouse was now a bakery-café and going from strength to strength. They'd even started to talk about those expansion plans... they'd taken a leap of faith and it had paid off, a hundred, a thousand times over. Yes, life was good, but it could be more.

It could be perfect.

Jack licked his lips. In the quiet and calm of their home, it was time.

"Do you remember me saying about taking a leap of faith?"

"About expanding the bakery? Yes, of course I do."

EPILOGUE

"Not exactly." Jack's heart hammered as he felt Rory shift and sit up.

"I don't understand," Rory said, looking down at him.

Jack pushed himself up and took Rory's hands in his. He'd had the words ready, rehearsed, worked out. He'd gone over them again and again, for weeks and weeks. The time had to be right to say the words that were straining at his heart, demanding to be said.

But there's never a right time, just like there's never a right time to expand the business... you just have to take a leap of faith...

Jack licked his lips again. A leap of faith. He just hoped to God Rory wanted to take that leap with him.

"What is it, Jack? You're trying to say something to me—what is it? You're starting to worry me."

"Christ, Ro. That's the last thing I want. I'm making a mess of this..." Jack thrust both hands through his hair. All his carefully prepared words fell away. *Say it, just say it...*

"A family," Jack blurted out. "That's what I'm trying to say, and messing it up. You and me, as parents. The biggest leap of faith we could ever take."

Rory stared at him and blinked hard.

"What?" he whispered. "Parents? Us? Me, a—a father?"

Jack swallowed hard as Rory slumped back into the

EPILOGUE

sofa, his body sagging as though all his breath had been punched from him.

"I've probably made you want to run screaming from the room." *Please don't do that...*

Outside, a car door slammed. A barking dog and a father laughing and calling out for his children to follow him. The distant blast of a car horn. And Jack's breath, hard and ragged in his chest.

Rory shook his head slowly, carefully.

"I don't want to make a sudden dash for it. I never would," Rory said, at last. "I mean, I can't pretend I'm not surprised, shocked even. It's not something we've ever talked about."

"I know it's a crazy idea, and you're probably thinking what the hell, and—"

Jack's tumbling words fell silent as Rory placed a finger against his lips. He stared into the warm, rich brown of Rory's eyes, his heart spiking as he saw not shock or fear or disbelief, but excitement.

"Crazy? It's madness, but I've always thought sanity was overrated."

"What? So you—you'd do it? Really? You really want to—"

"Take that leap of faith? Yes, Jack. With you by my side, I'd always take it and never think twice."

"Come here," Jack croaked as he pulled Rory into a hard hug.

EPILOGUE

He was shaking, every part of him trembling. Rory's hands rubbed circles on his back, calming and soothing, Rory doing for him what he'd done for Rory so many times before. Thoughts tumbled through him, running as fast as a river in flood. A new and bigger business, a new and bigger house, one to bring their baby home to.

His and Rory's baby.

The kiss they shared was long and lingering, each taking time to taste the other. Jack sighed into the warm sweetness of Rory's mouth that had little to do with the soft, rich wine they had drunk. The sweetness was all Rory, all love, and the life they would build with their family.

Jack eased himself away and stood, holding his hand out to Rory.

"Leap of faith?" he asked.

Rory smiled, placing his hand in Jack's as he stood

"Leap of faith."

Jack nodded, happy and content beyond all words, as he led Rory, his husband, and the man he loved more than he could ever say, through to their bedroom, closing the door with a soft click.

ABOUT THE AUTHOR

Thank you for reading, I hope you enjoyed Rory and Jack's Christmas wedding story as much as I enjoyed writing it. If so, I'd appreciate it if you could spend a minute or two to post a short, honest review. I'm an indie author and reviews are vital, they really are our life blood.

Why not sign up to my mailing list? Each month, I send out an up-date on what I'm working on, books I read or listened to in audio format and would recommend, events I've been to, and all kinds of nuggets I think you might be interested in. If you want to hop on board (and you can jump ship at any time by unsubscribing) as a thank you I'll send you a free 13,000+ word story.

You can sign up at:
www.aeryecart.com

You can also connect with me here:
www.facebook.com/aeryecartauthor

twitter.com/aeryecart
instagram.com/aeryecart

Just a little about me...

I love all kinds of MM romance and gay fiction, but I especially like contemporary stories. Born and raised in London, the city is part of my DNA so I like to set many of my stories in and around present-day London. I write at home, in the gym, in cafés - in fact any place I can find a good coffee!

ALSO BY A E RYECART

CONTEMPORARY GAY ROMANCE

DEVIANT HEARTS

Captive Hearts*

Radical Hearts

Perilous Hearts

*also available as an audiobook

BARISTA BOYS

Danny & Jude

Stevie & Mack

Connor & Ash

Bernie

URBAN LOVE

Loose Connection

The Story of Love

Corporate Bodies

RENT BOYS

Release

All series novels can be read as stand alones

HOLIDAY & SEASONAL

A Kiss Before Christmas (Rory & Jack #1)

An Easter Promise (Rory & Jack #2)

Company for Christmas

STAND ALONE

Imperfect

Printed in Poland
by Amazon Fulfillment
Poland Sp. z o.o., Wrocław

53795113R00141